CW00507341

THE AMERICAN COLLECTION 13: HER LUCKY NUMBER THIRTEEN

Dixie Lynn Dwyer

LOVEXTREME FOREVER

Siren Publishing, Inc.
www.SirenPublishing.com

A SIREN PUBLISHING BOOK
IMPRINT: LoveXtreme Forever

THE AMERICAN SOLDIER COLLECTION 13: HER LUCKY
NUMBER THIRTEEN
Copyright © 2016 by Dixie Lynn Dwyer

ISBN: 978-1-68295-706-6

First Printing: November 2016

Cover design by Les Byerley
All art and logo copyright © 2016 by Siren Publishing, Inc.

ALL RIGHTS RESERVED: This literary work may not be reproduced or transmitted in any form or by any means, including electronic or photographic reproduction, in whole or in part, without express written permission.

All characters and events in this book are fictitious. Any resemblance to actual persons living or dead is strictly coincidental.

Printed in the U.S.A.

PUBLISHER
Siren Publishing, Inc.
www.SirenPublishing.com

DEDICATION

Dear readers,

Thank you for purchasing this legal copy of *The American Soldier Collection 13: Her Lucky Number Thirteen.*

Sometimes in life we can perceive different things in different ways. Perhaps associate a number with bad luck, or a date with a bad memory and forever that number or that date remains in our head as negative.

Nalia has been through a traumatic experience. Yet, she embraced the desires, the need to be trained and prepared in case someone attacked her, and never expects to use that training to save her life. She associates the number thirteen with emotional days that changed who she was after each time. She considered herself on her own with no real family or connection of belonging.

Meanwhile in actuality, everything happened for a reason and ultimately that stubbornness she always had, the desire to be exactly like her father, to be prepared, to be smart and to survive on her own all came into play and saved her life. When she meets her men and falls in love with them, she thinks they could be bad luck too, but learns quickly that the things she used to look at as bad luck or in a negative fashion are actually good luck and ultimately her destiny.

Please enjoy Nalia's story as she struggles to believe that good things can happen to a woman like her, and the men of team 13 are her lucky charms after all.

Happy reading.

Hugs!

~Dixie~

THE AMERICAN SOLDIER COLLECTION 13: HER LUCKY NUMBER THIRTEEN

DIXIE LYNN DWYER
Copyright © 2016

Prologue

Karlicov Lenvick took position in the back of the auditorium. He did what he did best. Remain in the shadows as he kept a watchful eye on Nalia. He could see her mother, Danella, sitting alongside her husband, Raymond, waiting for Nalia's name to be called. Karlicov's daughter was graduating from grad school with her MBA. She'd already established herself in a firm here in Chicago and they offered her a great position with an excellent salary. He knew all about it.

He clenched his teeth as he thought about how much he loved her. How much it sucked to have to give her up in order to protect her from his lifestyle and the choices he was forced to make. When he and Danella fell in love, it had been a mistake from the start. Her family were enemies with his. But that conflict went back a hundred years and to a time and a people none of them even had a connection to.

But that was the Slavic way. To hold a grudge so strong that it would stand the test of time. He had no choice when he broke things off with Danella. It was separate or have both women taken from him and killed. The one man who knew of their existence held that information over Karlicov's head.

He sighed. Cornikup was no longer a threat. He knew that and disappeared, he was misguided, and his power was weak. Especially since Karlicov worked for Nicolai Merkovicz, head of the Russian mob.

In that moment Nalia's name was called out. He still felt sick every time he heard her last name, Nalia Sharp. It was Danella's, but it could have been worse. It could have been Raymond's. An average guy, with an average job, working as an accountant for an upscale business firm. It was Raymond's pull that got Nalia the interview and job, not Karlicov's.

The clapping continued as fellow students cheered her on as well as her parents.

He was shocked when Nalia looked right at him. His heart skipped a beat. His pride caused tears to fill his eyes. She knew all about him. She knew why they couldn't have a relationship. She was more like him than even Danella wanted to accept. Nalia was strong, smart, determined and well trained, because he'd told her all about him and why he couldn't be her father.

He stepped back behind the column as Danella looked over her shoulder. She wouldn't see him or recognize him. She forbade him to be near his daughter. She was still angry for the way they parted and angry that he saw Nalia on her thirteenth birthday and told her about his existence. Little did Danella know that Nalia was getting into trouble, hanging out with the wrong crowds and about to engage in a crime against one of Cornikup's main operations.

Karlicov had to intervene thanks to Storm and some inside information to Nicolai.

Instead of hating him and wanting to defy him, Nalia told him that finally things made sense. Her desires, her need to be empowered and take care of herself. She begged him for some contact, for instruction to defend herself in case anyone ever found out she was in fact his daughter. Nalia was stubborn, but also a young woman who knew what she wanted and went after it. She was fearless, and that fact would get her into trouble or even killed if she didn't learn control and patience. He lost the battle in denying her. He loved her with all his heart and he had to do whatever it took to protect her even from afar. What he hadn't expected was for her to fall in love with Boian.

His heart ached at having to make them go their separate ways. He watched as the ceremony was beginning to conclude and he headed out of the auditorium and down the hallway to the exit doors. He did what had to be done. Boian and his brothers, Viktor, Chatham, and Dusty, were hardcore American soldiers who nearly died serving their country but also had blood connections to Nicolai. Karlicov wouldn't have trusted any other soldier to teach his daughter self defense, weaponry skills, use of various weapons and other survival skills, especially since she took so well to it all. It made him proud, but also fearful that one day she could have to use it.

Boian wasn't happy about having to stop training Nalia. Although nothing happened between them, he could see the love in Boian's eyes and that in Nalia's. When Viktor showed up too Karlicov knew where this was headed. He didn't want her to have this life. He didn't want his daughter to become an instant target and Boian understood. He took the order and he ended their training. She more than likely didn't need it anyway. Not as a professional businesswoman, not as Nalia Sharp.

* * * *

Nalia Sharp hugged her mother and then her father Raymond. They were smiling ear to ear and so proud of her. She had done it. Worked hard, completed her Masters, and was all set to start a new position at the business downtown in Chicago. She'd started her internship there as a freshman in college. The bosses took to her well and she had many fantastic mentors over the years. She was thrilled with her starting salary and already well on her way in competing for a higher position. She enjoyed helping out with people's businesses and coming up with better strategies and ways of making more money for them. She had a knack for numbers which got her in a bit of trouble in her younger years when she ran poker games and other things in the schoolyard. Never mind the small stint working the numbers racket betting on sporting events and collecting money from college students with bad gambling habits.

She chuckled to herself. If her mom only knew half the stuff she did, she wouldn't be so proud of her right now. Nalia glanced back toward the post in the back of the auditorium again despite knowing that her father already left. He took a chance coming here.

Her heart felt heavy. She wanted him to share these moments and to be by her side enjoying life, engaging in dinners together and talking about business and getting his feedback. But that wasn't going to happen. Instead she was forced to have those conversations with Raymond. A man who insisted on her calling him dad despite knowing damn well he wasn't her father. Raymond hadn't a clue who her father was, or at least Nalia didn't think he did.

She felt the loss of not having Karlicov in her life all the time. Instead he came and went, maybe left something for her somehow, like the necklace gift wrapped in a beautiful little box inside her locked car. How the heck did he do that? Better yet, why did she find that to be so cool?

She took a deep breath and exhaled. Her fantasies of being involved with the Russian mob and becoming an asset to their organization and working side by side with her father were like the forbidden fruit. Karlicov would never let her get close enough.

She hadn't spoken to him in months. He made it clear that they couldn't have a relationship. She missed seeing him. She missed all that training she used to do when she first started college. She swallowed hard and her heart still ached a little. She had been stupid. A silly girl who thought she could win over the heart of an older soldier, a member of some elite group of men she knew nothing about. Boian was everything a woman wanted in a man and then some. Drop dead gorgeous, dark blue mysterious eyes, muscles galore, tattoos, capabilities made up in stories and in the movies and so much sex appeal she had been ready to give him her virginity.

She felt her cheeks warm. She was silly in so many ways back then. Boian had been ordered to teach her everything from shooting a gun to self defense to survival skills. The sick thing was that she loved it all. She even fantasized about being a soldier in the Russian mob. Being one of the people that others were intimidated by and afraid of. It excited her, gave her a rush in so many ways. It was like her comfort zone but instead she was forced to be a professional woman in a business world made for normal people with normal families and average lives.

She wasn't normal or average. She was a fighter, a go-getter and had to use some of that determination to get where she was. But she couldn't help but to feel like she was wasted talent. She wanted more. She craved more, but Nalia knew her destiny was pretty much laid out for her. She wanted to be the unexpected, but her father put the botch on that fast and no one, no one but her mother and her knew that she was Karlicov's daughter.

"So, we have reservations in about thirty minutes at Ronaldo's to celebrate. My God, Nalia. I'm so proud of you," her mother told her and hugged her arm as they walked out of the auditorium and to the car. On the way out Raymond stopped short and she could tell he appeared upset.

"Give me a moment please, ladies? I'll meet you by the car," Raymond said. Her mother didn't look twice and pulled Nalia along with her toward the waiting limo. But Nalia looked over her shoulder and she spotted the man in the dark suit. Raymond looked scared and then kind of angry. She watched the exchange of words and then Raymond glanced over toward her and his wife then back at the man and nodded his head. The man in the dark suit kept a firm expression. Nalia's gut clenched. Who was that man and what did he want?

"Mom, who is that Dad is talking to?"

Her mom glanced that way. "Hmmm, I don't know. I don't think I've seen him before. You know your father, though. He knows so many people. He's working on some big deal at work. He's been in meetings the last few days and hasn't gotten home until the wee hours of the morning. It's something big. He keeps saying our lives are going to change." She hugged Nalia's arm.

"Your dad has been saying that since we got married. He's always involved with something," she added as the driver opened the side door for them to get in. Nalia watched as Raymond turned to head toward them and the man he had been talking to walked away. Raymond looked upset.

"Is everything okay, Dad?" she asked him as he got into the car.

"Fine. Let's get to the restaurant," he snapped and she glanced at her mother. Her mom touched his hand and he snapped at her.

"Don't, Danella."

"Is something wrong?" Danella asked him.

"Don't ask me about my business. You know the rules," he snapped again.

The rules?

"Why are you suddenly so angry with me?"

He turned to say something to her mother with his teeth clenched and such anger in his eyes it made Nalia question who he was right now. Her mom gasped and then lowered her eyes. Nalia held his gaze and he gave her an evil look before he turned away. She didn't like the feeling she had. Call it instinctive but there was just something about Raymond that got under her skin and often made her wonder why her mom fell in love with him. A few minutes of silence passed and then she saw him cover her mom's hand with his and then squeeze it. Her mom looked straight ahead, and Nalia wondered what was going on as her heart ached for her mother.

Nalia often wondered what she had seen in Raymond to accept his proposal when Nalia was in high school. Especially knowing her biological father and how handsome and powerful he appeared. When she asked her mom what she saw in Raymond, her first response was stability. That didn't seem right at all. But as Nalia got older she learned a little about falling in love and not being able to act upon it for other reasons. She knew she would never marry a man she didn't love. She would rather live a lonely life than one without true love.

An hour later as they finished up dinner and small talk, Raymond seemed a little less on edge. That was, until the waiter told him that the bill had been paid. Nalia's gut clenched. She hoped her biological dad hadn't done that, but one glance at Raymond as his eyes locked onto a man standing by the bar and she knew something was up. He was very attractive, and older. At minimum early forties. Raymond nodded.

"Who is that, Raymond?"

"An associate of mine."

"Well, that was very nice of him to pay for dinner. You know him from work?" her mother asked him. Nalia held the man's gaze and he smiled softly. She got a funny feeling in her gut and looked away. It was strange, she had men flirt with her all the time and ask her out, even ask her to bed, but she never bit. Things were worse because of the time she spent with Boian. She swallowed hard and then jerked, looking up as the man from the bar now stood by the table.

"Thank you so much for taking care of the check, Mr. Scarlapetti," Raymond said as he went to stand up and shake his hand. The man placed his hand over Raymond's shoulder, squeezing it.

"No need to get up. So, this must be your wife and your beautiful daughter," he said, glancing at Nalia's mom but then totally focusing on Nalia.

"Yes. Danella, meet Mr. Scarlapetti." She shook the man's hand and smiled. His suave, sexy ways seemed to get to her mother, too. Her mom's cheeks flushed.

The man moved around the table. "And this is Nalia," Raymond said as he smiled in an odd way.

"Nalia, it's a pleasure to finally meet you." He took her hand and brought it up to his lips, kissing the top instead of shaking it hello. She shivered a little, unsure how to read this man, friend or foe.

"I'm afraid I'm at a disadvantage, Mr. Scarlapetti. My father hasn't mentioned you before," she said and he released her hand and licked his lower lip as he looked her breasts over.

"Well, we go way back, and only recently started to do some business together. So I understand congratulations are in order. You're MBA. Very impressive. Smart and beautiful," he added and gave her a wink. He pulled back and then stood by the table.

"Won't you join us for a drink?" her mom asked and Nalia wondered why. The man made Nalia nervous. Especially the way he stood so close and seemed to inhale as if trying to infuse her scent into his nostrils.

"I have some business to attend to. But thank you for the offer, Danella," he said to her and nodded slightly.

"We appreciate the dinner," Raymond said.

"Well, sit and enjoy your drinks," he told them and then walked away.

"He seemed nice and very powerful," her mom whispered and then took a sip from her glass of wine.

"He is a very wealthy businessman. The kind of man a father wishes for his daughter to marry," Raymond said. Danella widened her eyes and Nalia felt her gut clench.

"Excuse me?" she asked him.

"Just saying, Nalia. Vincent is quite the catch. Did you not find him attractive?" he asked her and she felt so weird.

"Uhm, you have never asked me anything like that before, so don't start now."

"Didn't you?" he pushed, a little firmer in his tone.

"Raymond, Nalia is shy when it comes to those types of things. You know that," Danella said.

Nalia felt completely uncomfortable. Were they going to try and set her up? Did they think that now she'd graduated with her MBA and was set in a professional career that she needed a man by her side? Not happening.

"I need to use the rest room," Nalia said, and stood up. He looked like he was going to say something else and then her mother touched Raymond's arm and he glanced away from Nalia with daggers now toward her mother.

She took that moment to walk away. What in the world was that man thinking? He never asked her about finding a man attractive. She headed through the crowded restaurant and as she went to head toward the hallway leading to the bathrooms she couldn't get through the crowd by the bar.

"Excuse me, please," she said.

A tall young guy with a button down dress shirt smiled wide. "Hey, gorgeous."

He looked her over, checking out her abundant breasts in the designer dress she wore. She knew she looked good, but also classy. This guy was with a bunch of other guys who looked like Mafioso wannabes.

"I'm trying to get to the ladies' room, could you please move?" she asked him.

He licked his lower lip and then smiled. He turned and at first she thought he might ignore her but then he yelled out for the guys to move and at his voice and tone they parted and gave her the space to walk by them. Their gazes at her body as she passed between them didn't go unnoticed. Nor did the funny feeling she got when she passed by one guy who looked as big as a linebacker. His eyes were dark and evil and his dress jacket was open, revealing just enough of his holster for her to see the gun. Maybe they weren't wannabes. Maybe they were the real deal?

She got to the ladies' room and was relieved for the time being. She took care of business and then reapplied her lip gloss and wondered if Raymond would push about finding Vincent attractive. What was up with that anyway?

Her phone buzzed and she glanced at it once she pulled it from her purse.

She read the text message from Clarissa.

Ditch the parents and celebrate with us at O'Rielly's. We're down the block.

She chuckled. Her friend didn't need to twist her arm.

Give me twenty minutes.

Yes!!

Nalia chuckled and then looked into the mirror. O'Rielly's was a great place. A lot of the people who worked at the office hung out there. It was a go-to place for a lot of celebrations. She took a deep breath and then prepared to tell her parents she was basically ditching them. As she headed out of the bathroom she was surprised to see Vincent standing there. He looked her over.

"Everything okay?" he asked her.

She looked at him strangely. "Yes. Why wouldn't it be?" she replied.

"I saw you having a hard time getting through that crowd of men."

"I got through just fine," she said and started walking. She felt him take her hand and press close to her back.

"I'll walk you through this time," he whispered next to her and then she felt the second hand on her hip as he escorted her through the crowd of men. This time when she approached they all moved out of the way as their eyes landed on Vincent.

She turned to look at Vincent before they came near her parents' table.

"I could have handled that fine," she said, staring up into his dark brown eyes. He caressed her arm on one side and she instantly felt on guard.

"I thought otherwise, Nalia."

She had a bad feeling in her gut and she turned away from him, hoping he would just release her and not follow. No such luck. The moment they were close her father smiled.

"There you are," he said. He and her mom stood up.

"I'm going to meet some friends so I don't need a ride," she told them and then went to kiss her mother's cheek in hopes Raymond wouldn't question her.

"Where are you going?" he asked and she didn't look at him.

"Just down the block."

"We can drop you off," her mom said.

"Don't be silly. It's a warm night and only a block down the street."

She felt the hand on her waist and one on her shoulder.

"I would be happy to make sure she gets to her destination, Raymond, Danella."

Both Raymond and Danella smiled.

"That is so nice of you, Vincent," her mom said and then Raymond took her hand and pulled her close.

"Have a good night. We'll talk tomorrow," Raymond said and then looked at Vincent. She caught the change in Raymond's expression and wondered what that was about but then they were leaving and she was left with this very older, pushy, attractive man who seemed to set his sights on her.

She turned around to face him just as another group of people were leaving the restaurant. He pulled her close and she grabbed on to his forearms.

"I think you need looking after."

She stepped back once the people moved. "I'm fine on my own, Mr. Scarlapetti."

He squinted his eyes at her and that gut feeling went up a notch.

"Vincent. Call me Vincent."

"I think Mr. Scarlapetti will do fine, considering you're a business associate of my father's. Thank you again for dinner, but I'm heading out and don't need an escort." She started to turn and move but then felt him hold on to her snugly as he led her out of the restaurant.

"I disagree completely," he said.

As he led her outside and down the sidewalk she knew that something was wrong. She tried to dislodge his hold on her arm but couldn't.

"What are you doing? Let go of me," she demanded and then felt the gun against her side.

"Get into the car, Nalia." He walked her closer to the dark SUV and the man standing there holding open a door. She didn't want to get in. She wondered what this was about and thought of Karlicov. She swallowed hard, her mind bouncing in all directions. She needed to be smart and to give up no information no matter what.

Once she was in the car another three men were waiting. Three of them were men who had blocked her path while she was trying to get to the bathroom. That same playboy in the dress shirt licked his lips as he looked her over. They were all packing guns.

"What is this about? What do you want with me?" she asked. She was scared now. No one was saying a thing.

Their stares at her body put her on edge. She crossed her legs and kept her hands on her lap and thought about how she could escape. But they had guns. She wanted to know what they wanted and then Vincent placed his hand over her knee. She pushed his hand away and he gripped it tighter as two of the men across from her pushed their jackets open, showing their weapons. It was a sure sign she should cooperate.

Vincent ran his hand along her knee and up her thigh.

"I've waited a long time for this moment. Waited until I felt you were ripe for the taking."

She swung her head around to look at him as she pushed his hand away from her thigh. In a flash his hand went to her throat and he pressed her over the guy's lap next to him.

"Don't fight me on this. You're going to be mine. All mine." He squeezed her throat a little tighter and she could hardly breathe. He used his other hand to glide up her thigh, causing the material to stretch and begin to rip.

She was scared and confused. Raymond introduced this guy as a business associate. Was he just some wealthy rapist? A guy connected to some Mafia stuff or something?

His dark brown eyes held hers as he lowered and licked her lips. She wanted to spit at him but could hardly even breathe with his hand gripping her throat.

"You're young and need discipline. I get that. You'll serve many purposes besides my revenge on your father." He pressed his lips over hers and she tightened up and tried to resist him. His hold tightened and his hand moved from her thigh to her breast.

"What are you talking about? What did Raymond do? Is this over some kind of business dealing with him?" she asked, not understanding the man at all.

He cupped her breast and she tried to push him off of her but now the man whose lap she was halfway over took her hands and pulled them back. She gasped, tilted her pelvis and ass off the seat, and cried out in pain.

He kissed her again and then held her gaze as he stroked her throat with his fingers. "Not Raymond. Your real father. The one who is going to die tonight knowing that I have his precious daughter who I'm going to fuck until you're pregnant with my child."

"I don't know what you're talking about. Raymond is my father. Are you some kind of nut case?"

He lifted up and the guy released her.

"Your destiny lies in my hands, Nalia. I know Karlicov is your father. I know he watched you get your diploma tonight. Just as I know everything there is to know about you," he said and ran his hand between her thighs. She shoved them away and he struck her across the mouth. Before she could strike back her hands were grabbed and pulled behind her. They had her on her knees in the back of the SUV and Vincent grabbed her hair. He pulled her head back and she gasped.

Slowly he ran his hand down her shoulder and over her breasts.

"Cooperate, and the first time you have sex it won't be painful." He licked her bloody lip and then smirked as the SUV came to a stop.

Did he know she was a virgin? But how? How would he know that? How long had he been watching her? She felt sick, terrified, and she contemplated what she could do to get away from him.

The doors opened and they were in some underground garage of a large upscale building. He dragged her from the seat and before they could get to the sidewalk she heard the gunshots.

"Get down. Fuck," Vincent yelled out. More gunshots went off and people were shooting. She pulled from Vincent's grasp, forearmed him in the throat, and ran. She ducked down between the cars and then rolled under an SUV and crawled under two more vehicles trying to escape.

She peeked around the one car and saw her father. Karlikov was holding his chest. She saw the blood.

She ran to him and felt the bullet whiz by her head. She noticed the guy trying to sneak up from behind him. She jumped for the gun and as the guy prepared to shoot, she shot him, saving her father's life.

"Daddy. Daddy?" she whispered as she covered his chest and he held her gaze.

"Go. Go and hide, Nalia. Trust no one. Do not let these men get their hands on you." He shoved her back as he pulled the gun from her hands. Another few shots went off by his head and hit the car he was next to.

"Run now. Do as I say and hide. Don't show your face anywhere. Go! Go now!" he screamed at her and he shot another two men as they descended upon them. Nalia was crying, she was so scared. She looked at him one more time. "Remember the training. Remember," he said and she saw his face. She knew he was in pain. He might even die. She was angry, scared, confused but she did as he told her to do and she scrambled through the parking lot and into the night.

She wasn't sure where to go to. She needed things. She needed her bag, money but her apartment was across town and more than likely these men, whomever they were, had to be watching that place. She thought about her mother. She needed to warn her and warn Raymond. That man Vincent was evil.

She was running on pure adrenaline, making her way out of the city and to the residential area where her parents lived. She didn't know what to do, and felt panicked as she hurried to get to their house. But then she began to process what was happening. She cried for her father Karlicov, wondering if he were dead and what she should do. He prepared her for this, a moment, a danger she didn't think would ever occur. When she was younger she almost wished for a chance to use her new skills, but now the reality of maybe needing them didn't give her such a wonderful feeling. Instead it made her feel sick, and question her capabilities after all.

She gripped her head as she made her way through the development to her mom's house. It was pounding and she felt like throwing up. Her dress was torn, her lips swollen and bloody. She climbed the fence, hoping they were safe. It was an hour since she saw Karlicov. Did he make it? Was he still alive or did those men kill him?

She felt the tears roll down her cheeks as she made it across the yard. No one was around. She couldn't see in the dark but no cars were in the roadway in front or down the street. She headed toward the back door. Her mom rarely put on the home alarm. If they did then so what that it would go off? She needed to warn them anyway.

She got through the door and into the dark kitchen. It had been months since she had been here but she knew her way around. She needed to get to her mom's bedroom and then to her bag in the basement.

She headed toward the living room and heard the whimper. A light popped on and Raymond stood there holding a gun.

"It's me, Raymond. Just me. There's been trouble. That guy Vincent you do business with, he's after me. He shot—"

She turned to see her mother sitting in the armchair gagged and tied up. Her face was beaten and bloody. Nalia was shocked and angry. "What's going on?"

"Why couldn't you just cooperate? Why did you have to flee?"

"What are you doing, Raymond? Why?" she asked and started to walk to her mother.

"Stop. Stand still right there. They're coming for you and this will be done," he stated through clenched teeth.

"You're part of this?" she asked him.

"I made this happen. Are you kidding me? You think I didn't know your mother was a fucking whore who got knocked up by a Russian mobster?" he yelled at her and she looked at her mother who appeared scared with her eyes wide and bulging.

"I don't know what you're talking about."

"Save it, Nalia. You're as good as dead once you pop out a kid for the Scarlapetti family."

"Fuck you. The police will find out about this. You'll go to jail."

"No, you will. Because you just killed your father, a made man in a parking garage on the east side. Then you came here and killed your mother."

"What? I did not kill him or my mother."

"Well, your fingerprints are on the gun. They set it all up. Right about now Nicolai Merkovicz is probably finding out about how you killed his right-hand man, your father, and then your mother. You're on a hit list. You're as good as dead," he said to her, practically smirking.

She was shaking, she was so angry and confused. "I didn't kill him and I didn't kill my mother."

She jumped and screamed as he pulled the trigger and shot her mom.

"No. No!" she cried out and ran to her.

Raymond grabbed her hair and pulled her back as he pressed the gun to her head.

She couldn't believe this was happening to her. Her father was dead and now her mother, too. She was shaking and feeling helpless.

"I know everything about you. I worked your mother over all these years and finally got what was coming to me. I know your every move. I'm going to bring you to Vincent myself. You're going to fuck him. Give him the kids he wants to secure the bloodline and take over the territory he wants. Your piece of shit father killed Vincent's brother and cousin."

He lifted her up and started pulling her across the room. She glanced at her mom, her tears streaming down her face at the sight of all the blood. He killed her. She was dead and so was Karlicov.

Anger pooled in Nalia's belly. She couldn't let him get away with this. She wouldn't let Vincent either.

"No. No, I'm not going with you," she screamed at him and he struck her with the gun in the back of the head. She remembered her father's words. Run. Trust no one. She had to get away. She had to go into survival mode. She had to.

"You don't know everything about me. You know nothing," she screamed at him.

"I know you're weak like your mother," he said and when he lowered the gun to drag her she used one of the moves that Boian had taught her and got free. Raymond's eyes widened and she shifted and thrust her hand upward, knocking the gun from his hands. He grabbed for her and struck her repeatedly but she didn't give up. She fought for her life and countered his moves, wrapped her arms around his neck and her legs around his waist. He shoved at her, trying to get her off of him as he banged her body against the cabinets and then the curio closet in the corner of the room. Fragile pieces her mother collected over the years shattered and rained over them but she kept her grip and tightened, letting the anger, the determination to live shove her into action. She screamed and cried, thinking of how he killed her mother and how she now had no one and was going to become the hunted.

He fell back on top of her on the floor. She gasped, losing her breath but then held on tight. She couldn't let go. She needed to kill him and get away from here. He struggled to get free and she remembered her training and instinctively went for the move. She twisted and heard the crack. His body went limp and she released him, shoved him away, and pulled from underneath him.

She was shaking, she was so scared and sick. She looked at Raymond, eyes open. She'd killed him. She actually killed someone. Then came the anger again. Her father was dead, her mother, too, because of Raymond. She ran to her mother and checked her pulse then cried as she felt nothing. She wanted to die right here and end it all. She continued to cry and hold her face to her mother's arm, sobbing. Then she remembered her father's words.

Run. Don't trust anyone.

She jumped up and wiped her tears. She ran for the basement and went to the corner and the hidden spot in the back of the room no one ever bothered with. She shoved aside the old spider webs and dead insects. She reached inside and pulled out the two bags. Guns, money, burner phones, knives, and ammunition. She took a deep breath and stared into the old mirror, barely seeing her full reflection. Life was over as she knew it. She was on the run. She was all alone and Vincent Scarlapetti would one day die because of what he did to her and her family.

Chapter 1

"Where is she?" Karlicov asked as he slowly awoke in the hospital. He coughed and Nicolai was there to comfort him. He held his gaze with a firm expression.

"We do not know."

"What do you mean, Nicolai? How long has it been?" he asked and tried sitting up. He cringed from the pain.

Storm was there to help him. "Easy, Karlicov. You were shot twice and we all thought you weren't going to make it. It was touch and go there for a while," Storm informed him.

"How long?" he repeated.

"Thirteen days."

Karlicov closed his eyes. He had been under sedation, painkillers and in and out of surgeries for that long? "Fuck," he whispered.

"We have a lot of men looking, but she disappeared," Storm said to him.

He looked at Nicolai. "Nothing more to tell me? Nothing?" he asked and felt defeated. His poor, beautiful daughter was caught in the middle of some mess. Into the middle of the lifestyle, the criminal element he worked so hard to keep her out of.

"Cosivan, Boian, Viktor, Chatham, and Dusty have been gathering more information while also continuing to search for her."

Storm gave a wink. "Never seen those five quite like they are right now. By means they were not willing to share they gathered information on Nalia's reason for disappearing even from us. Seems that Vincent Scarlapetti was working with Raymond, and negotiated a deal to take your daughter. He wants revenge after you killed his brother and cousin. In his sick, fucked-up head he planned on taking Nalia and marrying her, then having a child with her to join blood lines. We believe she thinks that they framed your death on her, and the death—"

Storm stopped talking and looked at Nicolai.

"What? Of who?" he asked and looked between both men.

Nicolai held a firm, serious expression. "Danella is dead. Raymond killed her," he told him.

Karlicov felt the tears hit his eyes and his heart ached. He loved Danella. Had given up that love to keep her safe and look where it got her.

"I want him dead," he whispered.

"Already done," Storm replied.

"Who? Boian, Cosivan, and his soldiers?"

"Nalia," Nicolai said to him.

He closed his eyes and felt his heart ache. His poor, beautiful Nalia who he tried to protect and love from afar was forced to fight and to kill. He swallowed hard then felt the hand on his shoulder. He blinked his eyes open.

"She is strong, Karlicov. She believes that she's been framed for both murders and being hunted by all the top families. She's running on fear and will continue to do so unless we can find her before Scarlapetti's men find her first," Nicolai told him.

"Why is he still alive?"

"You know there are rules and proper ways to do things?" Nicolai said to him.

"Just as there are proper ways to seek revenge?" he retorted.

"We couldn't get close to him if we tried. He's disappeared and every little lead we've come across turns up nothing," Storm added.

"Then we wait and we find Nalia first and get her to safety."

"How do you suppose we do that since it seems no one was able to find her so far, and even if we did, she's so scared and thinks we want to kill her, so who would she trust?" Storm asked.

Karlicov looked at Nicolai. He held his boss's gaze and felt his heart tighten and his gut clench. Was it the right thing to do? Was he standing in the way of the inevitable? Look what giving up on his true love had cost him. Danella and now maybe even his daughter, too.

"Call them, Nicolai. Send them to find her and keep her someplace safe."

Nicolai nodded and he and Storm walked out of the room to let him rest.

* * * *

"Who is he talking about?" Storm asked.

"Cosivan and his men."

Storm whistled low. "Holy shit, I didn't see that coming. Is there something I should know about?" Storm asked Nicolai.

"As you know, Storm, Cosivan, and his four buddies were soldiers, Special Forces in the Corps before they retired a few years back. They had several missions that were close calls, but the five of them live for danger. They have troubled pasts and Viktor trusted them with his life. Cosivan and he go way back to when they were children. Dusty, also having some family in Russia loyal to my family, got into some trouble."

"Dusty isn't exactly a Russian name."

"It's short for Dustoyva. Viktor gave him the nickname and it stuck. Anyway, when they returned from war, and serving as Special Forces, they needed work to stay out of trouble and to keep the demons away. Viktor asked me if I could help them like I had helped him when he was young. He thought of them as his brothers, his family, and I could see how close they were. Viktor is my nephew, so of course I gave the men the opportunity to prove their commitment to the family. They've never failed to do so."

Nicolai understood too well what Karlicov was going through. Karlicov always knew he had a daughter. Nicolai didn't know he even had a daughter until three years ago, and when he, too, tried to find her and attempt to protect her, even if it was from afar, she had been taken and her mother killed. He had yet to find her.

Nicolai kept straight faced as they walked out of the building and to the awaiting SUV.

"You and Karlicov are close, too, like brothers so did you always know about Nalia?" Storm asked him.

"Karlicov had saved Nalia from getting into a bit of trouble when she was a teen. She found out about him when she was thirteen and then began to act out, get into some juvenile crimes when she was a kid."

Storm widened his eyes. "So Karlicov stepped in?"

"He had to. She was about to engage in a more serious crime and against property belonging to a Cuban gang. He confronted her, saved her before she could be involved and her friends that did the crime paid the price. It wasn't enough to scare her because all she seemed to want was her father's love and attention. Karlicov kept seeing her without her mother knowing and he had her trained."

"Trained?"

"In self-defense, weaponry, survival skills he hoped she would never need but felt compelled to have her prepared, just as Karlicov is always prepared."

"That's how she was able to get away, to defend herself and kill Raymond. Who trained her?" Storm asked.

Nicolai looked at him. "Boian did."

"Oh," Storm said and then licked his lower lip.

"Karlicov saw the changes in Nalia as she was starting college, getting older, more mature and the changes in Boian. He forbade Boian to ever see her again and the training was over."

"So Boian fell in love with her and she fell in love with him?" Storm asked and then looked out the window.

"You know as well as anyone about how dangerous our lives are. You make sure that you protect Aspen and when you begin to raise a family, you protect them with all you have. Our enemies will stop at nothing to destroy us."

Storm nodded.

"So this is a big decision by Karlicov to choose Cosivan and Team 13 to find her and protect her?" Storm asked.

"He knows that his fight to protect her from this life was a fantasy, and that now she will need the love and protection of soldiers who will do whatever is necessary to protect her."

"Team 13 are intense men, to say the least."

"They aren't any more intense than you and your men, and they are just as resistant to having feelings, to making a connection and showing any sort of vulnerability, just as you and your men are. It seems Karlicov is now wanting to condone a relationship if it were to happen between his daughter and Team 13. All we can do is hope she accepts them when they find her and she doesn't try to kill them before they can explain that she's safe and that her father sent them for her."

* * * *

Boian slammed the guy's head up against the wall in the office.

"Please. Please, I don't know where she is. I don't," the Slavic piece of shit replied.

Boian was losing patience. He knew these fuckers caused her to run. She had to be so scared and out of her mind with worry. Three more days and it would be thirteen weeks she was on the run. Thirteen fucking weeks. Boian was beginning to think she was dead or worse, that Scarlapetti had her.

"You know something. I know you fucking do. We've been watching this place. Four men just left thirty minutes ago. Where the fuck are they going?" Dusty demanded to know as he stood right by Boian. They were all beyond worried. From the moment they knew Nalia was in danger they all gathered together and planned on helping her. It had been too late when they got to her mother's house. Boian knew immediately that Nalia had killed Raymond. In that moment he didn't know why, but now, thirteen weeks later and they knew everything.

He shook the guy and pushed his gun against his throat.

"I will blow your fucking head off if you don't tell me where Scarlapetti's men were headed. Then I'll kill your whole fucking family," he threatened.

He was shaking, he was so angry and just as the disappointed feeling filled his gut and he was about to release his hold on this piece of trash the man shivered.

"They'll kill me anyway. They have my daughter and wife," he said and started to cry.

Boian squeezed him and lowered him slowly to the ground.

"Where are they going?"

"My family. Please. They have my family," the man begged of them.

"Tell us where they have them and we'll help if you know for a fact that those men know where Nalia is," Dusty told the man.

Boian released him, letting the man fall to the floor.

Dusty pulled out his cell phone.

"Send men to Costano Avenue, house number 16," Boian heard his brother in arms give info to the other men they knew. There were troops of them still on the hunt trying to locate Nalia and save her.

"Are they going after Nalia?" Boian demanded to know.

"Yes. Someone caught sight of her or someone who they believe is her. The jet probably is leaving right now."

"Where? Where are they headed?" Dusty demanded this time.

The man told them an address. Someplace in Sacramento, California.

Boian struck the guy, knocking him out before he looked at Dusty.

"He won't be able to warn them that we're on our way. Let's move."

Chapter 2

It was early evening and Nalia was heading back to the small trailer she rented. As she made her way across the side streets, ignoring the chaos of nightlife around her, she felt the hairs on the back of her neck stand up. Something was wrong. Someone was watching her.

It was crazy, but since the night her entire world turned upside down, she fell into this instinctual, protective mode and was more in tune to everything, even her gut instincts, than ever before. Her fears were now turned into anger. Anger at the man Vincent who caused all this damage to her life and who killed her father as well. She knew it would take time and patience to regroup, to plan and survive, but she was determined. Her father had warned her about the possibility of this day, yet she never really thought it would happen. She did train like the potential was a great possibility and thankfully so. She used everything Boian had taught her.

She swallowed hard. She thought of Boian a lot and of a time when things seemed so different. He was older, capable, a soldier. He seemed to have feelings for her one minute and the next was cold as ice. It was the making of some forbidden love story, but she was so young, inexperienced, and a danger to him and especially to her father. It gave her a little insight into the way of life her father led and in being part of a Mafia-like organization.

Yet, when she thought about the attraction she felt for Boian and the way she trusted him so much, she didn't care about the dangers of pursuing him. Thank God she hadn't kissed him or thrown herself at him like some lovesick nineteen-year-old. Although, look what not giving in to that attraction got her. Lonely, still a virgin, and now in the midst of danger Boian and her father tried so hard to keep her out of.

She shivered as that same feeling of being watched took over all other thoughts. She cleared her head. She had to stop thinking so much, but she was lonely, scared and knew at any moment Vincent, his men, her father's men and family could find her and kill her because they thought she killed Karlicov and her mother.

The tears burned her eyes. She was all alone and that was how she was going to live for however long she could.

She pulled her hoodie tighter, kept her hand on her gun and the hood down low over her face as she made her way around the back. Only a few months back she was wearing designer dresses, picking out clothes for her office job in the city and planning to attack the work place with vigor, enthusiasm and a determination to be a CFO within a few years. Now here she was like some criminal thug on the street, her manicured fingers chipped, the hands of a killer on the run.

She gripped the small bag of groceries tighter as she decided to make sure no one was indeed following her by taking the long route through the outdoor mall. She would pass the side bars on the strip and mix in with the crowds of people.

She finagled her way to the most crowded spot by the outdoor bar. There was a dark space covered by a partition that looked to be where servers went to grab items being cooked in the small kitchen. She moved into position, keeping her eyes peeled for anyone noticing her or approaching. She then reached into her small backpack and pulled out the other hoodie in grey. She put that one on and then threw on the sweats. It was so damn crowded no one seemed to look toward where she was or care that she changed her hoodie right there. She put the backpack back on under the hoodie after shoving the groceries into the backpack and tossing the bag.

It was enough of an alteration in her disguise to not make them look at her if indeed someone was watching her.

She hurried out the back open bar area, passing a small crowd of people laughing and enjoying their drinks. What she would give to go back in time and enjoy hanging out with her friends from college, and thinking that mobsters and murderers didn't exist She slipped past them, looking all around her as she snuck down along the side alley and to the side street before the trailer park. Her heart was pounding inside of her chest. Fear, loneliness, desperation were all emotions she was getting used to.

"Going someplace, Nalia?"

She jumped as the deep voice startled her and two men dressed in dark clothing now stood in front of her.

"Excuse me," she said and pretended to walk by. Then the gun was against her side and he shoved her hard against the wall.

Her palms landed against the bricks, stopping her face from colliding with the hard, rough surface.

"Let go of me."

"You're coming with us," the other one said. She felt the fear hit her gut. These were men who worked for Scarlapetti. She didn't run this far and hide this long to get caught now.

"Okay, I'm done. I'm tired of running," she said as she slowly turned and acted defeated.

The one guy lowered the gun and smirked.

"Easier than expected," he said to his buddy.

She struck her forearm hard against the man's throat. He coughed and released her and the other one raised his gun. She kicked it from his hand, using the other guy's shirt to grip and hold on to. It was a martial arts move she mastered well. The one guy went down hard and the guy she held on to she kicked in the crotch, sending him down to the ground before she turned to run.

Shots were fired from their position on the ground, missing her somehow. She heard yelling in the background, two more shots, and the pain in her side. She reached down and pulled her hand away as she ran. Blood. *Oh God, they got me.* She was running on pure adrenaline when she ran across the street right through traffic.

Horns honked, people screamed out but she ignored them and continued to run as fast as she could. As she got to the other side she slammed into a car. She hit the hood, rolled over and landed with a thump hard on her shoulder. The side door opened and a man looked at her with evil in his eyes. She rolled, pulled her gun, and shot him. His buddy shot back and she used the door to push against the car then returned fire, killing him. She gripped her side, looked around to be sure no one else was there to shoot her and she took off, and ran as fast as she could.

She needed to get to the trailer, grab her things, and disappear. They'd found her.

She hurried into the trailer after being sure that no one could see her. She climbed through the back window and felt the pain. As she got inside she ran to the bathroom and looked at the damage. A flesh wound, she thought, hands shaking and covered with blood. Thank God. It hurt so badly though and the blood wouldn't stop. She might need stitches and she couldn't get any. She couldn't go to a hospital. She grabbed the washcloth and pressed it against the wound. She knew she needed to leave. She had to get the hell out of there. She would worry about the gunshot later.

Her hands were shaking. They felt numb from pulling the trigger on the gun. She just killed some more men. *My God, will I ever be safe?*

She grabbed her things and knew she needed to hurry. The night was on her side, her only means of getting out of this town, this state alive.

She grabbed her things from under the bed and made sure she didn't leave anything behind. She took off out the side door and across the grass. Once again, she was on the run. When would she finally be free?

As she ran toward the wooded area and around the last set of trailers she screamed. Thick hard arms wrapped around her waist, holding her tight. She kicked and screamed and tried to grab her gun. It was removed from her and a heavy body had her on the ground and completely restrained.

"Nalia, you're safe. You're safe, baby."

She locked gazes with Boian. She widened her eyes.

"Don't kill me. Don't kill me, Boian. I didn't kill my father or my mother. They did. Raymond and Vincent did," she cried and saw four other men all holding guns and standing around them yet watching that no one else was coming.

Boian released her arms. He cupped her cheek. "We know that. Your father is alive, Nalia. We've been trying to find you for months. We're here to protect you," he told her and she felt the tears fill her eyes.

"He's alive?" she asked through blurred vision, the tears threatening to spill. She'd held them in for so long.

"Come on. We have to get out of here now." One of the other men barked an order and they all reacted, even her. Boian pulled her up and she cringed in pain.

"Follow us. The SUV is around the corner."

She fought to not show weakness. But Boian was there. He came to rescue her, to find her and tell her that her father was alive. Was he lying? She tried slowing down and he pulled her along. He held her around the waist as the adrenaline rush was beginning to leave her body. They got her into the SUV. They all piled in. Five men and her.

She panicked as Boian released her and she grabbed the gun he'd stuck in his waist and she turned it on him. She squatted on the seat ready to shoot and kill.

"I want to talk to my father. I need to know that he's alive."

"Calm down and put the gun away, Nalia," Boian whispered to her, hands in the air.

She shook her head, felt the tears roll down her cheeks. The gun shook in her hands. "No. Don't tell me what to do. I need to know he is alive and that you're not lying."

She glanced at the others, who didn't seem too concerned at all that she held a gun against Boian's head. In fact, they looked cold as ice and she felt the trepidation hit her gut. These men could kill her, she just knew it.

"Have I ever lied to you, Nalia?" Boian asked.

"I don't know these men. None of them. I don't know you, Boian. It's been years since I saw you so don't even try that shit with me. My father gave me orders. Get him on the phone now!" she screamed.

"Here." One of the men from the front handed over a cell phone. He put it on speaker.

"She can hear you, sir," the driver stated aloud.

"Nalia, put down the gun."

"Who is this? You're not my father. I want to hear from my father."

"They're waking him now."

"Who is this?" she asked.

"Nicolai Merkovicz."

She gasped.

"I take it your father at one point informed you of who I am. You are safe now. These men were assigned by your father to find you and protect you. He is alive, Nalia, and these men are now your guardians until further notice."

She covered her mouth with her hand.

"Here, someone wants to speak with you."

"Nalia?" She heard her father's voice. She gasped and started to cry.

"I'm alive. You saved my life in that garage. You've been so strong, baby girl."

She began to sob and turned the gun around and handed it to Boian. "Daddy, oh thank God, Daddy."

"I know, Nalia. Everything is going to be just fine. You did so good. You did as I said and you ran and didn't trust anyone. Now I'm asking you to trust Cosivan and his team." Her father coughed.

Her eyes widened and she felt afraid. "Are you okay? Daddy?"

"I need to rest. Trust them. Do as Cosivan and his team says. Do whatever Nicolai asks of you."

"Let the men take care of you. We have a plan for your protection," Nicolai said and then disconnected the call.

She covered her face with her hands and slumped back into the seat.

Boian held her on the waist, gave a gentle reassuring squeeze, and then covered her knee with his hand. She gasped and pulled her legs away.

"What the hell?" Boian said as he looked at his hand. She saw the blood and so did the others.

"Who got hit?" the one man across from her asked. He had very blond hair, and despite being dressed in all black, he looked large and muscular.

"None of us," the one across from her said as he continued to stare at her.

"Someone was shot?" the man driving asked.

"That would be me," she whispered.

"What?" The question came from the man driving. He was huge and his forceful tone made her jump.

She felt the hand on her thigh as the one large man in front of her leaned forward.

Boian clutched her chin. "How bad and where?" he asked as the other guy began to feel around.

She grabbed his hands. She felt an instant tingling and she locked gazes with him. "A flesh wound, on my side, I'm fine," she said to him.

He leaned closer and grabbed her hoodie, unzipped it then pulled up her shirt as he spoke to her. "How the fuck do you know it's only a flesh wound?" he demanded to know as he lifted her hoodie and tank top up higher. The other guy next to him leaned forward as he pulled something out.

She stared at him very seriously. "It isn't my first," she told him. The truck went silent.

"We can stop if we need to but it wouldn't be smart. We have an hour's drive to the private airport and the jet," the man driving said from the front seat.

"I'll be just fine," she said to the guy who was so close to her she could see the definition in his cheekbones, the light blond streaks in his hair and his firm lips. The other guy used the light from his phone to shine on her skin.

"Fuck," he whispered.

The blond across from her cupped her cheek and brushed his thumb along her lower lip. "Are you certain?" he whispered.

She couldn't believe it. He was so good looking. So sexy and older like Boian. She felt an instant attraction which was completely ludicrous considering the current situation. She nodded her head.

"Here's the first aid kit. I'll hold the flashlight," the other guy said. She locked gazes with him as Boian helped her to lean back.

They were silent and she winced a few times as the guy cleaned up the wound to check it out. His hands felt so warm, so gentle against her skin. He was big. They all were, and a feeling of claustrophobia began to simmer in her gut. The space was confined and the air palpable.

Boian wiped the blood from her swollen lip, and stared at her with a firm expression, and those striking dark blue eyes of his. She couldn't look at him. Those old feelings, the attraction was instantly back and she knew nothing could come of it. She was a different person now. These last months had changed her. She jerked when the man in front of her cleaning her wound brushed against the underside of her breasts. She locked gazes with him.

"Thank you. Whoever you are," she whispered.

"I'll make the introductions," Boian stated. "This guy right here who's so good with his hands is Viktor. The one with the flashlight is Dusty. In the front passenger seat is Chatham and the boss, our leader, Cosivan is driving."

So the commanding one with the deep voice she immediately responded to was their leader. Interesting.

She nodded toward them and could tell even in the dark cab of the SUV that they were very dangerous, important men. She knew instantly that they were Boian's team members, American soldiers who served together in war, and were Special Forces. These were the men her father hadn't wanted her to ever meet. Why was Boian here now? Her father changed his mind and she wondered why. She couldn't feel excited to know that Boian was here. He was just doing his job. She understood that. But she had feelings for him. She had thought about him so much over the last several years. That's why her father sent him. He knew she wouldn't have trusted anyone else and she probably would have shot them. A deeper feeling of loneliness struck her core.

Then she felt the fingers under her chin and Boian tracing her lip with his finger. "I was so worried about you." She felt the tears reach her eyes.

"Why did my father send you, of all people?" she asked and saw his eyes squint at her directness. There was no room for pussyfooting around. She was direct, and she wanted answers. She earned that right by fighting for her life and taking lives of people out to get her.

"Your father knew that my team and I would be the best ones to protect you. He felt that you would trust us, because…because of the fact I trained you years ago," he said, and she couldn't help but to think that wasn't the complete truth. Or maybe she hoped Boian would say that he insisted he be the one to find her because he still cared for her and didn't care what anyone said. That was some silly girl fantasy and hope. This was reality. Death, violence, and being on the run for her life. She had to be smart and keep in control.

"Raymond said you were going to kill me. That they planted the gun to be found that killed Karlicov and my mom. That the Russian heads would issue an order to kill me. My father said to me to trust no one and to run, so I didn't use the burner phones. There was no one to trust," she said and then blinked the next tears away.

She felt the heat against her side and looked down to see Viktor caressing her skin. She locked gazes with him.

"You're not alone anymore. Your father sent us to watch over you and protect you. That's exactly what we're going to do," Viktor said to her.

Her heart felt heavy, and her body ached as the pains, the bruising and the possibility that she was indeed somewhat safe filled her mind. They were five large men. Men she really didn't know, but was asked to trust. She didn't think she could ever trust anyone again, and show weakness. She definitely couldn't show weakness when it came to Boian. She had to be strong. Her past life was behind her and her future was something she needed to look at a day at a time. That thought had her heart aching and her closing her eyes and hiding the emotion these men would surely see. Nalia learned fast that showing weakness gave others power over a person. No one would have power over her ever again. No one.

* * * *

Cosivan nodded toward Boian once they were settled in on the jet. Boian looked over at Nalia. She kept fighting falling to sleep. She was exhausted but still in defense mode despite them assuring her that they weren't there to kill her or take her back to Chicago. Even though she'd talked to her father and to Nicolai she was still on the defensive and untrusting. He knew it would take time. She had gone through hell and then some.

He watched as Boian patted her knee. Cosivan felt his chest tighten. Thirteen damn weeks the woman remained hidden and on the run. He was beyond impressed, and especially with her ability to kill when needed. It upset him that she was forced to take lives in order to save her own. But knowing what those men did for a living and how brutal and barbaric they were, he felt no remorse and hoped that Nalia wouldn't either.

"Yes?" Boian said to him as he took the seat beside him.

"How is she?"

"In pain but fighting it. She won't let us look at her other injuries, but I think they're just cuts and bruises on her shoulder and back. Viktor assured me that as long as we keep changing the bandage and applying the ointment then the risk for infection on her hip where the gunshot wound is will decrease."

"I'm sure we can have someone with medical skills to evaluate her if you're that worried."

"I trust Viktor, and I trust you. There's no need to make our presence in Salvation known. Viktor and you know what you are doing. You both took care of us how many times in the service and with worse wounds than Nalia's. Plus, add in your skills, and if need be you can do stitches if she needs them."

Cosivan nodded his head. He couldn't help but recall the close calls they did have, but they always had one another's backs. Even Viktor, who came from this Russian mob business. It had taken him the longest to trust them and for them to trust him.

"Do you think she's a flight risk once we land?" Cosivan asked him.

"I don't believe so. We were close, once, and hearing her father's order over the phone and reassurance helped. Plus, she knows who Nicolai is. She wouldn't go against him," Boian replied and then looked back at Nalia. She was watching them with hooded eyes. She didn't trust them despite them being here to protect her.

"That was years ago, Boian. She's older, more mature and more experienced in life."

"She needs me. She needs all of us."

Cosivan took a deep breath and exhaled.

"I'm trying to determine the best location for the hideout. Storm assures me that their friends have a definite secure location and that no one will ask any questions. We don't even need to leave the house. Supplies will be delivered as needed. Plus, Aspen will be nearby along with her men."

"Whatever you think. You're our leader. I respect your decisions."

"I think someone needs to keep a clear head here. We're not out of danger."

Boian squinted his eyes at him. "I'm keeping a very clear head."

"Are you?" he asked, raising one of his eyebrows up at Boian.

Boian ran his fingers through his hair and then massaged the back of his neck.

"I'll do whatever is necessary to protect her. I'm never leaving her side again. Never," he told him and then stood up and walked back over to Nalia.

Cosivan locked gazes with her, his expression firm and protective of his brother. She wasn't one of them. She wasn't part of the family because Karlicov didn't want her to be. He hoped his brother would be careful. This was a serious time and a blood war could take place wherever Nalia was located.

* * * *

Nalia gasped, went to jump up from her seat and Viktor held on to her.

"You're okay. You're safe," he said firmly with his hand over her belly and hip. She blinked her eyes open and licked her lips before she swallowed hard and cringed.

"Here, take a sip of this." He offered her a bottle of water. She reached for it with shaking hands and he covered her hands and helped her to take a drink. His chest tightened. She was so scared and he knew it would take a long time until she wasn't so skittish.

She looked around the cabin of the plane. He followed her line of sight straight to Cosivan and Boian and then to Chatham and Dusty who pretended to be sleeping. He knew his team members, and they were never fully asleep. "Where are we?" she asked him and then moved in her seat and winced.

"About thirty minutes away from landing."

"I need to use the ladies' room," she whispered.

"I'll help you," Viktor replied and undid his seatbelt and then reached over and undid hers. He couldn't resist sliding his hand along her waist and to her hand. There was just something about her. He stood up and helped her to stand next.

"I've got it," she whispered, looking up at him with those gorgeous dark blue eyes. She was sweet, beautiful, young, and he carefully released her. She started walking and held her side then let go. She was being tough again. He showed her where the bathroom was and then walked back to the front.

"Should we check the wound again?" he asked with concern.

"When we get to the house in Salvation," Chatham said to him and then he waited for her to emerge.

"What's the plan, Cosivan? Will we be able to protect her there?" Viktor asked.

It was so crazy, but in these weeks that they searched for Nalia he learned so much about her. They dissected her past, her schooling, the job she worked at and had been offered a fabulous package at upon obtaining her MBA. She was smart, sexy, and had the whole world at her fingertips. He almost felt jealous, because she had the opportunity to explore her options.

His future was set for him. When he was sixteen, his father, Jordan, was murdered right in front of him. He didn't think twice as he ran for his father's gun, turned, and shot Turner Hanze. He was a big shot in the criminal world in their world of Russian mobsters. As shocked as everyone had been to learn what he had done, he hadn't been shocked at all. He hardly even reacted. The anger at watching his father die at the hands of such a monster did something to Viktor. It had been his uncle, Nicolai, who took him into hiding, who taught him everything he needed to know about being a made man and a soldier for the Merkovicz dynasty.

Over time, his heart hardened and he was forced into another situation that made him have to kill someone he thought of as a friend. The trust was broken. He was broken, and he joined the military in order to evade being knocked off himself. Then he met his brothers.

He glanced at them as Cosivan talked about the house, the property he chose to provide security and a safe house for Nalia while further plans were made to handle Scarlapetti.

Then Nalia returned and she gripped the wall and looked off kilter. Boian got to her first.

"Whoa, slow down, honey. Are you feeling okay?" Viktor asked her as she held on to Boian.

She shook her head. "I think I need something to eat," she whispered.

"I'll grab some stuff," Viktor said and he was surprised at the sort of jealous feeling he had at seeing her cling to Boian. He could tell Boian was protective of her. He had been a madman from the first phone call about her being in danger. He had been hard to control as he questioned people and became more and more violent to get his answers. He knew that Karlicov stopped Boian from training her and seeing her. It had been instant. One day he was meeting her and the next he was forbidden to make any contact with her. Even then, Boian was a monster for quite some time. He changed. He closed up and now, meeting Nalia, and knowing all he learned of her, he could see why. She was perfect. She was beautiful, sexy, smart, skilled, and a survivor just like each of them. She was also off limits. Karlicov chose them because they were the best at what they did. He knew that his daughter would trust Boian and eventually them too because of the time they shared years ago. It was a strategic plan. Viktor just had this feeling that sometimes plans backfire and watching over Nalia had all the basics for disaster.

Chapter 3

Nalia was grateful to have finally showered and changed her clothes. She barely remembered the town they drove into and then the outskirts of it. She kept dozing in and out. She hadn't realized how tired she was. She remembered seeing the word Salvation and then another sign earlier for a place called Tranquility. Salvation was where they were staying. Someone met them at the airport terminal and followed them all the way to the town and even to the house. McCallister was the name or something like that. The house was huge, on a ranch-like setting with lots of land. It was secluded, and she wondered why they chose such a place. It made her feel like an easy target, yet the thought of being surrounded by strangers was worse. She knew that they knew what they were doing. This was Boian and his team's job. She swallowed hard. She was a job for them. They were on protection detail and it bothered her.

She couldn't help but to watch the men when she had a chance. Her attraction to Boian was as strong as ever. She never forgot about him or about the way his hands felt on her as he taught her so many defense moves. Nor the way he clutched her shoulder, laid his body over hers as she learned how to shoot many different firearms. She remembered the scent of his cologne and the gentleness in his touch, but also the firmness of his tone. When he gave an order it was intimidating besides arousing.

They were all pretty damn attractive and filled with muscles. It was their eyes, their expressions and body language that separated them from any other men she had come in contact with in her life. That hardness was a barrier of sorts. She knew they killed people.

They did it in the service as Special Forces and they did it as soldiers in the Russian mob. Surprisingly it didn't shock her or make her feel sick or scared. It was all a means of survival just as killing had been for her.

She looked at herself in the mirror and saw a similar hardened expression in her eyes. She killed, too.

Her heart pounded inside of her chest and that sick horrible feeling filled her gut. She didn't think. She reacted. Those men she killed were going to kill her. They were going to drag her back to Vincent so he could rape her and force her to bear his children. How sick was that? How demented. Was this what men did to women on a regular basis to seek revenge? She didn't understand it. She couldn't process it until she thought about Cosivan and the whole team of men she now shared this house with.

She knew before the full question finished in her mind that the answer was no. They could never do such a thing. But other men were evil. Others like Vincent who sought revenge were capable of such things. Things a normal, civilized human being like herself would never even imagine doing.

She felt her chest tighten. She was capable of more than even she thought she was capable of. In the midst of danger, living on the run with killers on her ass, she, too, planned her revenge against Vincent for killing her father. She thought of ways to infiltrate his home. To allow him to take her to bed and to think her submissive and accepting to his control and then she would slit his throat or put a bullet in his head. She cringed and swallowed the terrible taste in her mouth. She didn't even care about dying at that point. She even imagined her choices as his men came to find him dead or as she killed him then tried escaping and they caught her. She hadn't cared. She would have wanted to die because her mother, her father, the only true family she had, were dead.

She shook the thoughts from her head as she gripped the sink and thought about the bullet that came so close to penetrating deeper. The wound was bleeding again and she reached for the dark towel to press against it. Her breasts poured from the black lace bra she wore. She had thrown on her panties and blue jeans with the rips all over them. They were her comfort jeans, or at least they used to be. There were no comforts now. Maybe never again.

She jumped as she heard the knock on the door.

"Nalia, are you okay?"

Boian.

"Yes. I'll be out in a minute. I'm just trying to stop the bleeding," she said and the door pushed open and he and Viktor were there.

She gasped, pulled the small towel over her chest, and turned away.

"Let us see," Viktor stated and she swallowed hard and glanced at their images in the reflection in the mirror.

"Let me put something on first."

"No. We can see better and you won't get blood on anything and ruin your clothes," Boian stated firmly and like a man who knew what he was talking about. She kept the washcloth over her breasts best she could but she was well endowed and as she felt the hands on her hips she realized her pants weren't zippered up and they were slightly lowering. They probably could see her black thong panties, too. Oh God.

She swallowed hard.

"What's going on in here?"

Dusty? Jesus.

"We need more bandages and some of the antiseptic. It's still bleeding," Viktor stated.

"She may need stitches after all," Boian said, standing close to her with his hands on his hips. He looked so angry.

"I'll be okay," she whispered, her voice sounding sexy and breathless and she swallowed quickly.

Viktor's warm, large hands glided along her skin. One was on her hip and the other she felt tracing her tattoo. She glanced down at him.

"Sunflowers?" he questioned her.

Boian leaned closer. His arm grazed her breast as he gripped the counter with his hand to lean on, his face inches from her head. She felt his warm breath against her skin. "Her favorite flower," he whispered. She turned slightly to the right. His lips were so close to hers. All she had to do was lift up slightly and she could feel them against her lips. But she stopped herself from being some foolish inexperienced woman with a crush on the sexy gangster that trained her years ago. It would never work. Her father would never allow it. He chose Boian and his team of capable men because he knew she could trust Boian. That was the bottom line.

As he pressed a little closer and she felt his finger graze over the trim of her thong, Dusty came back.

"Here, I got a bunch of things. Cosivan said he can do the stitches if need be."

"He may have to," Viktor said as he began to clean out the wound.

"What? No way. Does he even know what he's doing?" she asked in a panic.

"I can assure you I'm so good you won't even see a scar."

She gasped at the sound of Cosivan's voice. She turned and saw him in the doorway along with Chatham.

Thank God the bathroom was very large with a sitting area and a separate shower and bath. She felt claustrophobic though, with men this big in here surrounding her.

"Let me see." Cosivan's strong tone had her tightening up. When he touched her hip she dropped the towel and then went to bend to get it off the floor but his hands firmed. "Stop moving," he ordered. She gasped and then placed her arm over her bra and breasts in an attempt to cover some of herself up. He locked gazes with her through the mirror.

"You need a few. I'll get things ready. We have some supplies, but it may be a bit painful," he told her, his hand on her hip. God, he was a hard scary man. His deep, angry expression with his eyes squinted, his jaw firm added to the intimidation factor. He had very short, crew cut strawberry blond hair. His eyes looked dark blue and he had this aura about him that put her on edge and made her immediately accept his power and control. There was no denying the man's ability to lead and to get whatever the hell he wanted.

"Is it necessary? Can't we wait a few more days?" she asked.

"No," he said and then stepped back and started heading from the bathroom giving orders.

Boian caressed her hair from her cheek but not before looking at her breasts. "You can trust him," he whispered and the tears filled her eyes.

She shook her head and lowered it, but then Viktor placed his palm over her belly and held her gaze in the mirror. "You can trust him. He saved lives more times than I care to remember." Viktor then stepped away and walked from the room.

"We'll help you," Dusty said to her.

"Let me put on a shirt," she told them as she turned and reached for her tank top.

"No need. It may get bloody," Chatham said and she stared at him wondering if he were telling the truth and then he wiggled his eyebrows at her. "I personally like the view and don't want to cover it up quite yet."

Boian gave him a smack. "Nice, Chatham," he said and pushed him from the bathroom.

She felt her cheeks warm and her belly tighten. This was bad, really, really bad. How the hell was she going to get through this?

* * * *

"How are you feeling?" Boian asked Nalia as she downed another shot of vodka.

"I told you that I can hold my liquor. The numbing agent is enough. I'm not weak, or a baby," she snapped at him. The others were all there too as Cosivan prepared what he needed to do the few stitches.

She stood up and lost her balance. Boian grabbed her around the waist.

"I think you are ready now," he said to her and she glared at him. *God, she's so beautiful.* He wanted to kiss her, to hold her in his arms and explore her luscious, sexy body. She wasn't some high school girl and a freshman in college that he was training. She was voluptuous, smart, professional and a grown woman.

He held her close and cupped her cheek and she leaned closer like she would kiss him and he turned and cleared his throat.

"Let's get you down on the bed," he said.

She shoved him away.

"I can do it," she stated firmly. Obviously insulted that he didn't let her kiss him. He knew if she did then he would lose control and he would take her, make her his and probably get killed by Karlicov for doing it.

Cosivan gave him a mean look. Chatham and Viktor stared at her body. Dusty gave him a sympathetic expression.

She reached for the hem of her tank top and pulled it up over her head and threw it right at him. She lay on the bed and one look at her body and then his team and he could see they found her to be just as sexy and desirable as he did.

Viktor reached over and tucked the sheet into the waist of her jeans.

"I need to undo this," he said to her as she held his gaze.

"Do it," she said firmly but kept her eyes locked on Boian.

* * * *

Cosivan took in the sight of Nalia. She was all woman from head to toe. Her belly flat and trim, her breasts abundant and exploding from the bra she wore. The sight of the black string to her sexy little panties was enough to make him come in his pants. One look at the others and he knew they were in a heap of trouble. They were all attracted to Nalia. They felt protective instantly. They had been obsessed with her for the last several months as they tried to find out everything they could about her and who she was, who she hung out with, even who she dated. Which was no one.

She was never with a man and that led them to believe she was a virgin. If what their sources said was true, it was another reason why Scarlapetti sought her out as a means of revenge against Karlicov. He could take her virginity and taint her. He could rape her, force a child upon her, and then kill her. It made him so sick and angry he knew if and when he got the order, he would kill Scarlapetti himself.

He stared at her little dainty sunflower tattoo, her sexy hipbones, and then the gash to her side. She was so damn lucky the bullet hadn't lodged into her side. There would be no way of protecting her in a hospital and with cops around asking questions. They would have knocked her off in no time.

"Easy breaths," he whispered to her as he set up the needle and prepared to begin stitching her skin.

He pressed a hand over her belly and she swallowed hard, glancing at him.

"Trust me," he told her and she held his gaze and started to look panicked.

"He's very good. We're here to protect you and ensure you don't feel any more pain," Viktor told her.

She glanced at him and took a deep breath.

"I can handle it," she said and looked toward Boian. Whether she realized it or not, she continuously looked to him for support, for direction. Cosivan almost felt a little jealous.

"Here we go," he whispered. She tightened lightly on the first pinch of needle to skin.

Boian held her hand. Viktor placed his hand on her shoulder. Dusty and Chatham watched over them.

"Why didn't you come back, ever?" she asked Boian.

He looked away.

"I want to know. Was it that I was so young, unattractive, boring and too simple for you, a man who has seen so much and is so worldly? I know my father probably felt I was ready and trained enough, but you felt something back then, didn't you, Boian?" she asked and tightened again on the second stitch.

"Nalia," Boian whispered.

"Forget it." She turned away.

Cosivan didn't look away from her skin. He heard her words and he could tell that Boian had feelings for her. She tensed again as he made the third and final stitch. He was trying to be careful and to ensure there wouldn't be a bad scar. Knowing her father, Karlicov would have that taken care of and no one would ever know she had been shot.

He made the small knot and then reached for the scissors but Viktor was there to hand them to him. He cut the end, then added the ointment before securing the wound with a bandage.

"You did great, Nalia," he said to her.

She glanced at him and gave a small smile. "Thank you, Cosivan," she whispered and then Viktor pulled away the sheet from her jeans. Boian reached for the clasp to cover her up so they could no longer see her black panties but she pushed his hands away.

"I am more than capable of handling things myself. You can leave now," she said to him. Boian opened his mouth to say something but then stood up and walked out of the room.

Cosivan got up and cleaned up all the materials he used and needed. Viktor was next to her.

"You should take some pain medication."

"I'm fine," she replied.

"There's no reason to feel any pain. We have stuff here. In a little while you're going to feel the ache from the stitches," Cosivan said to her.

"I don't mind pain. This is nothing compared to other painful things. So don't worry. Just leave me alone to rest."

Viktor placed a throw blanket over her. Then he and Cosivan walked out of the room.

* * * *

"You care about her," Dusty said to Boian.

Boian took a slug of vodka and then placed the glass into the kitchen sink. He sat down at the table and ran his fingers through his hair.

"It's understandable. She's beautiful and sweet, plus strong, too. She's not like other women," Dusty added.

"No, she isn't. But she's Karlicov's daughter and we're here to protect her," he replied.

"She still has feelings for you," he added.

"Because she's inexperienced and young," Boian replied.

"Maybe—"

"Stop, Dusty. None of it matters. I can't have her. We can't have her," he said to Dusty and Dusty swallowed hard. Cosivan, Chatham and Viktor walked into the kitchen.

"What do you mean we can't have her? We went over this a few years back. I thought it was decided that a relationship with any woman was pointless," he said to Boian.

"I said that then because I was forced to not see her again. When I knew she was in trouble I wanted to take off like a madman and kill anyone in my way to get to her. Cosivan stopped me and calmed me down. Like always. Each of you has helped me in so many ways. In all honesty I was grateful her father asked me to stop the training. I wouldn't have been able to be the man she needed or would have wanted. Not alone."

"That's not true. You're more than capable of caring for her on your own. Besides, look where you not being around her eventually got her. In the middle of danger," Chatham said to him.

Boian exhaled.

"We're trained to be obedient. To not question an order and especially one issued by our bosses and our team leader. Some things can't be helped. Sometimes fate steps in," Chatham added.

"You're the playboy tough guy fucking women left and right and whenever you damn well please. This is different, Chatham. I'm not talking about fucking some fine piece of ass. I'm talking about the future. I can't do that. I can't trust myself to handle it alone," Boian admitted.

Dusty cleared his throat. "We all have our problems. Our weaknesses and hang-ups. But together we get through them and that isn't going to change," Dusty said next.

"That's exactly what I mean. Together we get through things. Together is all we know. One team, one family. American soldiers first and then soldiers of our professions next. Where does she fit in with a life like we have?"

"Where does she fit in now? I for one think she's pretty damn fucking perfect. You're a lucky man, Boian," Dusty added.

"No, I'm not. You want to know why?" he asked them. They stared at him. "Because when I thought about her being mine back then, about caring for her and protecting her, I thought about doing it with each of you by my side."

"What?" Chatham asked.

"It's exactly what I'm saying. Sharing her. Making her ours. I think her father knew that was a possibility, too. It could never happen, not with him working for Nicolai, not with her mother marrying that guy and wanting Nalia to have a normal life, not one tainted by violence and the complications of a ménage relationship."

"It would never work now either. We've made too many enemies. Her life would always be in danger," Viktor added.

"Look at Stone and his brothers. Things seemed to work out perfectly for them," Dusty added.

"She's Nicolai's daughter and he basically picked Stone and his team for her. Get your heads out of your asses and remember why we are here and who we work for," Cosivan joined in.

Boian exhaled and then leaned back in the chair.

They all went about preparing something for dinner as Nalia rested upstairs.

* * * *

"Nalia, there's no one left to come for you. You got them all killed. Your father, your mother, the men who risked their lives to find you. You're all mine to do as I please with."

Vincent ran his fingers along her body. She was tied to the bed, exposed to him and shivering with pain and fear. She felt battered, weak, broken.

"No. No, get away from me. No more. Don't touch me anymore," she screamed at him and he straddled her body. He was naked and she was pulling on her bindings trying to get free. She screamed for help and struggled against the bindings on her wrists. He grabbed her throat and stared down into her eyes with his dark evil expression.

"I say when it's over. I own you, Nalia. Now and forever."

She screamed at the top of her lungs and cried out in pain as he assaulted her body, took what he wanted despite her begging for him to stop hurting her. Her heart was racing and felt like it could leap from her chest, and then she couldn't breathe and she felt more hands on her and couldn't see. It was so dark suddenly but she knew others were touching her. Oh God, no. No!

* * * *

"Nalia, please wake up. Please wake up," Boian begged of her but she was lost in a nightmare and flopping around on the bed begging for help and for the pain to stop. She was calling out Vincent's name and screaming.

Cosivan grabbed her from Boian and pulled her against his bare chest. She was practically naked, only wearing a flimsy tank top in black and some kind of boy shorts panties that barely covered her ass. He held her arms up against his chest so she wouldn't break the stitches in her side. "Nalia, open your eyes. Open your eyes now," Cosivan demanded as the rest of the team stood there with no shirts and pants on not even zipped up. They ran to get to her, guns drawn and ready for action.

She blinked her eyes open, the tears spilling from her eyes. She was sniffling, gasping for breath.

"Easy. You're safe," he told her and Boian caressed her back. She jerked away from him and clung to Cosivan. He pulled back.

"You're okay. It was a nightmare," Boian said to her as he knelt on the bed behind her.

She swallowed hard and lifted her head up to look at Cosivan. He was pissed off and angry, but also way too aroused and feeling protective to remain holding her against him.

"It's okay now. Let's make sure the stitches are okay," he said and lowered her to the bed, rolling her to her back. In this position her breasts pressed against the sides of her tank top and appeared to be escaping from the sides. It was pulled up to her belly and he placed his palm on her belly to look at the bandage. Carefully he lifted the bandage up and was relieved that no blood seeped through and no stitches were torn. She shivered beneath his touch. He held her gaze. "You're safe, so remember that."

She nodded. He started to sit up and she grabbed Cosivan's hand.

"What's wrong?" he asked. That sadness and insecurity in her eyes pulled at his heart. A heart he conditioned to be Teflon tough.

He reached up and glided a finger along her jaw. She covered his hand with her own and it felt so feminine and delicate.

"You need us to stay?" he asked. Not even thinking first but including them as a team. It kind of made him stop a moment to process what came naturally. He was just as needed as his brothers. He couldn't face handling Nalia alone, not in an intimate setting like this and her so vulnerable and scared.

She looked around them and then rolled to her side, taking his hand with her and forcing him to lie down behind her. He got comfortable and wrapped her in his arms as he inhaled her shampoo and the scent of her skin. With every breath he took Cosivan began to understand why Boian was having such a difficult time keeping away from her. Nalia was special indeed.

* * * *

It quickly turned into a nightly thing. Whoever brought her up to bed was the one to stay with her and hold her at night. Chatham lay with her now and knew exactly why his brothers were feeling so on edge and snappy. They desired Nalia just as he did. She was sexy, curvy, and sweet. During the day they kept busy talking, asking questions, and learning more about her and her training. She spoke very little about how she survived and not at all about how she got away. She wouldn't talk about her mother either. She excused herself to walk out of the room. Which led to him coming in here and holding her now.

Chatham figured with time she would heal and maybe open up to them.

"You don't have to stay here with me," she whispered, looking away from him.

"If you don't want me here, I'll leave," he whispered and he begged inside that she wouldn't tell him to go.

He heard her sigh and had a feeling that she didn't want him to leave.

"Nalia?"

"Stay, Chatham. I feel better when one of you is here watching over me." She chuckled low. "Isn't that so silly?"

He ran his hand along her waist and under her t-shirt. She felt warm, feminine. "Not silly. You're being honest," he added.

She was silent a moment. "It must have something to do with you being soldiers. You know, that whole protective thing. Having capabilities to do things and survive," she whispered and her voice cracked. She was having a hard time, and he couldn't help but to think she was suffering from traumatic stress. She went through hell from what they gathered.

He moved her to her back and he lifted up to lean on his forearm as he used his hand to caress under her shirt. "You are safe with us, and in our arms probably the safest," he teased then smirked. Her cheeks turned a nice shade of pink and she closed her eyes and turned away.

He reached up and clasped her chin between his fingers. Her dark blue eyes were glossy and filled with emotion and even fear. She was so beautiful, his heart was racing.

"You think I'm young and inexperienced. I get that. You don't know what I've done. You all think I'm so different from you. But I'm not," she said to him.

He looked at her lips and into her eyes again. "You are different. You're beautiful, untainted, sexy, smart—"

She turned away from him and rolled off the bed. He stood up too and she looked out the window.

"Nalia?" he said her name and she didn't look at him.

"You can leave, Chatham. I want to be alone," she whispered and he hesitated, felt compelled to go to her, pull her into his arms, and kiss her until she was limp and accepting. Then he thought of the team, and of Boian. It wouldn't be right. They needed to talk about this again and about making Nalia their woman. He wanted her, too, and right now it was painful leaving her alone and heading downstairs away from her.

* * * *

"Where's Nalia?" Cosivan asked in an angry tone.

"Upstairs. She wants to be alone."

Cosivan squinted his eyes at him.

"What happened?"

He explained. Cosivan rubbed his jaw. He couldn't help but be concerned. Maybe it was a good thing that he just got off the phone with Storm.

"I just heard from Storm, and was giving him an update. Him, his team and Aspen are coming over tomorrow for dinner."

"Is that such a good idea?"

Cosivan took a deep breath and released it.

"She's closing up and she isn't happy. It may be a good idea for her to be with another woman and talk, and also for us to talk with Storm and the guys. We need to go over a plan of action. Figure out how long we'll need to remain in Salvation. We have other obligations being taken care of temporarily, but we may need to alter those arrangements."

Cosivan could tell that Chatham wasn't acting like himself. He would be lying if he dismissed the change in his men as being caged up in this house for the last three weeks. It was more than that, and he was feeling it, too. Nalia was becoming more and more important to them.

"Then we need to gather some things to cook and prepare," Chatham replied.

"You might as well organize it with Dusty and then contact Zin. They're planning on bringing whatever we need tomorrow and for the next week, so we don't need to leave this estate."

"You think the town isn't safe?" Chatham asked.

Cosivan chuckled. "Are you kidding me? Storm and their law enforcement friends have this place crime free. How often do you see that?" he asked Chatham and Chatham smirked.

"Okay, then maybe some other excursions would be smart for her sake and sanity as well. We can ask Aspen about things to do tomorrow."

"Sounds good," Cosivan said and then watched Chatham go. He looked up toward the stairs and felt the need to go check on her. But he shouldn't. He didn't want to send the wrong message or give in to this attraction they were all feeling. They were stuck in a large house, five men and one sexy, attractive woman who was vulnerable and needy. It was the ingredients made for disaster. Maybe someday excursions would be a smart idea after all?

Chapter 4

"So, how are you really holding up?" Aspen asked Nalia.

Nalia looked out toward the back of the house.

"I'm fine."

"Yeah, right. Listen, there's something you should know about me, considering we have some things in common."

"In common? Like what?" Nalia asked.

"Like having a blood connection to the Russian mob that has placed us in danger and made us do things we never thought capable of but actually were pretty good at. I know your pain and your fears. I also know you don't want to hear it but time will make it all better. It will get less scary at night, and you'll gain back a little bit of confidence each day," she said.

Nalia looked across the room at Boian and Chatham. She let her eyes roam over their bodies and how they stood there looking so sexy and capable. A glance to the right and she spotted Cosivan, Viktor and Dusty. They were talking with Storm, Zin, York, Weston, and Winter, Aspen's other men.

"Ahhh, I think I see what's going on," Aspen said and then took a sip from her bottle of water.

"Hmm?" Nalia questioned, and turned back to look at her.

"I understand that Karlicov had Boian train you at some point," Aspen said.

"Yes."

"He cares about you a lot."

Nalia exhaled and then took a sip from her water bottle. "He was accepting an order from his boss. Just as he and the team were assigned to me now," she replied.

Aspen chuckled. "They have each looked over here several times in a matter of minutes. They don't watch you like men who don't care," Aspen said.

"I do believe they care. They take their jobs very seriously and I'm certain it's because of the dangers if they didn't." She played with the bottle and then moved to place it onto the table and winced slightly.

"Nalia, are you okay?" Boian asked. Everyone looked at her. She nodded her head.

Aspen smiled.

"You care about them, too."

"They're very kind and resourceful. I was feeling pretty fearful when I first met them. It was an intense moment."

Aspen smiled then looked at them. "They're not bad to look at either," she said and Nalia was shocked. Aspen chuckled.

"Got it bad, do ya?" she asked Nalia.

"How did you meet your men?" Nalia tried changing the subject.

"Oh, a similar way to you and yours. They always looked out for me and thought of me as a little sister. Or so I thought. So while I was seeking revenge against a man I figured out was responsible for my abduction and near sale to a prostitution ring overseas, they rescued me. But not before I took down said man's entire business operation and wound up abducted again and nearly died. It was pretty traumatic. But, my men are Navy SEALs, and they have connections," Aspen told Nalia.

Nalia was shocked. "Some men tried to sell you as a sex slave?"

Aspen nodded her head and then placed her hand over her belly. "I wouldn't be here right now if it weren't for my men."

"But you've accepted them and they have accepted you, Russian mob ties and all?" Nalia asked.

"Well, they did have a choice of giving it all up and trying to live a normal life, but they worked so hard and considering my ties to Nicolai as well, it was a no brainer. I love doing business. I'm good at it and have been able to keep right on top of things here in Texas as well as in Chicago."

"That's amazing and you seem truly happy."

"You could be, too," Aspen told her.

Nalia shook her head and then re-crossed her legs. "I'm afraid that isn't the case. Karlicov is the only family I have left and I'm not even sure where I'll stand with him when all this is over."

Aspen sat forward and put her water bottle down. "What do you mean where you stand? He sent his best men to help find you and save you. He purposely assigned Boian and Team 13 to find you and protect you."

"Team 13?" Nalia asked.

"That's their known name in the circuit," Aspen told her and Nalia chuckled.

"Well, that's just another reason things wouldn't work. Thirteen isn't exactly my favorite number. It's always signified bad luck and negative connotations."

"How could that be? I find the number thirteen to be quite lucky and especially when dealing with a baker's dozen," Aspen said and winked. Nalia smiled. She was enjoying Aspen's company and appreciated her support despite not knowing her until today.

"Well, I was born on Friday the 13th and my mom went into early labor and nearly died while delivering me. On my thirteenth birthday I found out about Karlicov by accident when he dropped off a gift, like he did year after year, and realized my father was alive and hadn't died in a car accident like my mother always told me. It was then I was told to forget he existed because he was a dangerous man and if anyone knew I was his daughter then they would try to hurt me."

"My God, that must have been terrible," Dusty said, joining them eavesdropping.

"What did you do?" Aspen asked her.

Nalia snorted. "What any teenager would do. In the next several years I acted out. It got to the point where I would do things in hope of getting my father to accept my existence and perhaps even allow me to be part of his life despite the fears of danger. Then it became a need to just see him in person, even if it were to reprimand me or warn me to stop hanging out with a certain crowd."

She chuckled. "I was doing some pretty crazy stuff. One night, while planning to rip off this small warehouse that had some electronics and stuff, my dad caught wind of the situation somehow and intervened. He saved me from getting killed that night from some Cuban drug dealers. It was also the night he confronted me about why I was getting into trouble, especially since my mom met Raymond." She swallowed hard.

"He married your mom soon after?" Storm asked. Now the others were gathering around them, all taking seats. Nalia hated to be the center of attention but she also felt challenged by the emotions and being put on the spot. It was crazy but she always felt it necessary to prove herself, despite the pain.

"By nineteen Karlicov decided it was important for you to learn to defend yourself and to be able to survive and escape in an emergency," Boian said to her and everyone.

"I was more than ready," she stated firmly then smirked as she recalled first seeing him and feeling intimidated but also interested.

"You had your moments, Nalia," Boian added.

"That's amazing. That you two met years ago and that Karlicov chose you, Team 13 to find Nalia, and protect her," Aspen added with a smile.

"Like I said, thirteen has been a very unlucky number for me," Nalia said.

"Actually, it's pretty interesting that you bring up the number thirteen. As I recall, we found you exactly thirteen weeks after you escaped from Vincent's hold, and it was on the 13th of the month," Chatham said with his arms crossed in front of his chest.

"I was also shot on that day, and was forced to kill four men in order to survive," she stated firmly.

"Perhaps in that moment when they found you and brought you into their safety that it was a change in luck for you, Nalia. A positive step in the right direction and to freedom," Zin now added to the conversation.

Nalia was silent as she looked at the men.

"Speaking of the situation, what else do you know about Raymond, Nalia?" Winter asked, changing the subject. Nalia noticed that Aspen seemed disappointed. She was pushing for Team 13, as they were called, to be more than just Nalia's bodyguards. However, Nalia wasn't stupid. She saw this for what it was. Not a story with a happy ending like Aspen's and her men who once saw her as a baby sister. No, this was a means to an end, and an unknown future for Nalia who would be alone and abandoned.

She looked at Winter, who was indeed a very attractive man just like the others on his team. She swallowed softly.

"I don't know much, just that my mom thought he was stable, reliable and safe. I suppose it was the better route to go than to continue and lust for my father, a man who wouldn't reciprocate that love. But then again, look where it got her," she said straight faced.

"Raymond definitely covered his tracks well. After investigating him we believe Scarlapetti and he had dealings about a year before he married your mother."

"Raymond said he worked her over to get to the point of trusting him. He showed no remorse, no emotion but an expression of a man on a mission when he shot my mother in the head."

"Jesus," Dusty whispered and Aspen covered Nalia's hand with hers.

"I'm so sorry, Nalia," Aspen said. Nalia felt her eyes tear up but she quickly pulled her hand from Aspen's and went straight faced again.

"Raymond got what he deserved. Crazy thing is, my mother wound up in danger anyway, despite Karlicov's belief that he was protecting her by staying away from her. Pretty ironic, don't you think?" she asked. Everyone was straight faced.

"I think we should start cooking up those steaks. What do you say, Storm?" Cosivan interrupted. His command and control of the situation was obvious as everyone stood up and Weston and York helped Aspen stand. Nalia noticed how Weston kept a hand over her belly. Aspen caught her expression and smiled.

"I just found out a few days ago that we're expecting."

Nalia smiled. "Really? Oh my God, that is wonderful. Congratulations," she said to her and Aspen took her hand and squeezed it. She walked with her and Weston and York followed them out of the living room.

"You can have it all, Nalia, despite their fears and insecurities as well as your own. It's fate the way you all have come together in a time of fear and dire need to have some sort of connection and reason for existence. Mark my words, thirteen is indeed your lucky number," Aspen said.

Nalia looked straight ahead and saw everyone working together to prepare for dinner. Even that wasn't something she was used to. Maybe Aspen had a point, but right now, Nalia's lack of trust and belief in happiness wasn't budging.

* * * *

"What's standing in the way? Karlicov? Nicolai? You need some sort of permission, or acceptance? Because I can tell you right now, Cosivan, that woman is interested in you and your team and you're interested in her," Storm said to Cosivan.

Cosivan clenched his teeth. "We don't need fucking permission, it just isn't smart. Not now, not when she's in the danger she is. Hell, Storm, she hasn't even spoken to us about how things happened and what Scarlapetti said and did to her. We only found out about Raymond shooting her mother in front of her just now, like you heard her say. The shit she went through, I can't even imagine. She's vulnerable right now. You heard what she said. She killed four men, and we know from the trail of blood in her path to freedom that she killed more than that."

"Damn," Storm said aloud and glanced back toward the house. Cosivan followed his line of sight and could see Nalia in the kitchen with Aspen and the others.

"Let me ask you something. Do all of you want her, and I mean want her and not just for fun," Storm asked him. Cosivan squinted at his friend and held a firm expression.

"Okay then. Don't be stupid. We were idiots with Aspen. We treated her like a sister as we watched her live a life, get flirted with and touched by other men and then be threatened by very bad men. We could have lost her a second time. Now look at us. We're made men. We're soldiers, and in about nine fucking months, fathers."

"What?" Cosivan asked and Storm nodded then took a slug from his bottle of Bud.

"Yup. Just found out a few days ago. We're fucking doing it all, man. We can protect her, our family, one another, together and have all the things we never had or only dreamt about. So what that she's Karlicov's daughter? He chose you guys because he knew Nalia would trust you. He isn't stupid. Maybe he's even smarter than the six of you," Storm said and raised one of his eyebrows up in challenge.

"You think he wants us to make her our woman?"

"I think he knows that her safety, her existence will always be in jeopardy and danger because she's his daughter. He knows what happened to Danella. He left her to avoid her being in danger and still she wound up dead because of him. If you care for Nalia then see where it leads. If you're unsure then continue to deny anything is going on. The last thing you want to do is break her heart and make her feel more alone than she already does right now."

"Alone? She has all of us here with her, protecting her."

"Cosivan, she lost her mother, thought she lost her father, and doesn't even know what Karlicov's intentions are once this is over. There's nothing concrete that she can count on right now but those survival skills Boian taught her. She needs more. We all do," Storm told him and Cosivan nodded his head.

Chapter 5

"We're not going to find her. Not now. She took out several men on her own and disappeared into thin air. It's obvious we underestimated her abilities," Romeo Lapella said to Vincent.

Vincent ran his hand along his jaw. They were sitting by the bar on the patio in a private estate along the beach in Florida. He had been lying low but then his associates guaranteed his safety and security as he told them what his intentions were. To take ownership of prime realty in Chicago as well as the casino businesses there and further south. There was enough money and business to spread out amongst various crime families, but he didn't want the fucking Russians getting their hands on anything.

"All I can think of was that Karlicov had her trained, or she isn't alone but has guards."

"She wasn't seen with anyone. Our sources that night a month ago proved for several days she was alone in that trailer. She's the daughter of that fucking dirty Russian sick bastard. He taught her everything," Romeo said and took a sip from his mixed drink.

"I don't give a fuck how long we have to wait. I will get my hands on her. How about Karlicov? Any means of getting to him to finish the job?"

"Not happening. He's highly covered and Nicolai has sent out some threats of his own."

Scarlapetti widened his eyes. "He's threatening me? That dumb fuck doesn't know who he's dealing with. Our family's been around long before those dirty fucks started moving in on our businesses. Damn fucking micks screwed things up years ago by sharing shit with them and giving up territory. All this 'play nice' shit to keep the cops off everyone's asses. Fuck that and fuck them. Figure something out, Romeo. I want her in my possession. I'm willing to wait. I can be a patient man. When she steps back into Chicago or someplace accessible, grab her. The window of opportunity will be small. Make sure the men know what she's capable of. I don't care if she's beaten and almost broken. Just bring her to me, alive. I don't want to accept Cornikup's help. He'll want Nalia for himself," Vincent said to him.

"Why does Cornikup want Nalia? He's hardly even involved in any business in the States anymore. All his ties are in Russia and the Ukraine."

"I think it's personal and goes way back between him, Nicolai and Karlicov. My need for revenge is more recent. I no longer have my brother and cousin because of Karlicov. I won't rest until I take away the only thing he has left and cares about. His daughter. Do whatever is necessary. I want her, and I won't stop until she is in my possession."

* * * *

Boian sat beside her on the couch. He couldn't get the fact that she witnessed her mom's murder out of his head. He felt the need to be here for her despite feeling the conflict of what he and the others really wanted. To make her their woman. She sat next to him, ripped jeans, pale blue t-shirt with a V neckline that exposed the deep cleavage to her abundant breasts. She smelled incredible, too. He leaned a little closer.

"What you told us all last night, about Raymond and what he did, it stuck with me." He placed his hand over her thigh. "That must have been terrible for you. What made you go to the house anyway?" he asked her.

She swallowed hard as Chatham walked into the room. He brought in a couple of bottles of water then took the seat next to her other side.

"My father told me to run and to not trust anyone. Vincent knew Raymond and I foolishly thought that he wasn't part of the plan to take me. I felt the need to get to him and my mom and warn them. I guess I didn't think fast enough or put together what my gut warned me about at the restaurant where I first met Vincent."

"What do you mean?" Chatham asked her. She looked at him and then away from both of them.

"We were celebrating at the restaurant, Raymond, Mom and I when Vincent paid for our dinner. He had his eyes on me immediately and every ounce of me felt on guard, yet, I knew that sensation. When a man shows interest and his eyes roam over a woman's body. I blew it off as another guy flirting with me," she said and Boian felt his jaw tighten. He hated to think about men wanting her but she was sexy and attractive.

"He came over to the table, Raymond introduced him as a business associate, and then he stood next to me and really focused on me. Anyway, when he left Raymond pushed me about dating, marrying a man as perfect and wealthy as Vincent and that was what any father would hope for his daughter."

"What?" Chatham asked, squinting at her.

"I was so pissed off, you have no idea. I gave him an attitude and went to use the ladies' room. He never asked me anything about my love life, about dating or anything, so why now? I should have known it was like some sort of plan. I mean if I was stupid and went all gaga over Vincent's good looks and sexy style plus him being wealthy, then God knows where I would be right now," she said.

Boian didn't want to think about that, or about how Vincent Scarlapetti could have gotten his hands on her, manipulated her, and taken her to his bed willingly. He felt even more responsible for her and for not pushing about his feelings sooner and instead being a good soldier and hiding them.

"How exactly did it go down? How did you figure something was wrong?" Chatham asked her.

"My friend called to hang out and meet down the street. I had just come out of the ladies' room and these guys had blocked my path earlier. I recognized them from the car later when Vincent forced me at gun point. I knew they were carrying, saw their weapons, but still was being stupid. Like why would any of that matter or have anything to do with me? So when I came out of the bathroom, Vincent guided me, used the guys bothering me earlier as an excuse to escort me to my parents. I made the excuse about leaving and hanging out with friends and the next thing I know Vincent is offering to walk me and I'm refusing. Then he's pressing a gun against my side and I'm forced into the SUV."

"The same men were in there that you saw in the restaurant?" Chatham asked.

"Yes, and when Vincent told me what he wanted and I tried to resist, they showed their guns and held me down."

"Held you down?" Boian asked, teeth clenched. She lowered her eyes.

"It doesn't matter now. I was shocked at the things he said, and disgusted and frustrated that I couldn't stop him from kissing me and touching me and telling me exactly what he planned on doing to me." She sat forward and Chatham and Boian reached for her, but she leaned against Chatham. Boian felt his gut clench. She was purposely keeping him away from her because she thought he didn't care about her in that way. Hell, he was in fucking love with her.

"That must have been pretty scary. How the hell did you escape?" Chatham asked.

"We arrived at some building in a parking garage, and when they opened the door and we started getting out, shots were fired. The one guy went down, and as I turned I heard more shots and I shoved against Vincent, slammed my forearm into his throat, and ran. As I saw where the shots were coming from I saw my father and he was shot," she said and Chatham caressed her arm as he held her close.

"My father told me to run and to trust no one, and that's what I did."

"So you ran to your mom's house?" Boian asked.

She looked at him and sat up straighter.

"I wanted to warn Raymond and her about his friend Vincent." She looked away from them.

"What happened next, Nalia?" Chatham asked her.

She shook her head and stood up.

"No, I don't want to talk about it. I don't need to talk about it," she said as tears rolled down her cheeks. She wiped them away quickly.

"Nalia, it might help to talk about it," Boian said to her. He never wanted her to feel such pain. To see Raymond kill her mother, and then to have to fight for her life.

Chatham leaned forward and then Boian saw Dusty enter the room.

"What's going on?" he asked, his eyes squinting with concern over Nalia. They all cared so much about her.

"Nothing. What are you doing? Maybe we can see what's for lunch," she said and held on to Dusty's arm and walked with him out of the room. Dusty looked at Boian and Chatham and Boian nodded, letting him know it was okay. They left the room.

"Damn, she's hurting," Chatham said and stood up.

"She pulled away from me and went to you," Boian said, standing now, too.

"She's upset, and obviously pissed off because you keep pushing her away. It's getting to the point where none of us want to push her away. We have to make a decision," Chatham said to him.

"Something has to give. I'm losing the ability to resist her."

* * * *

Nalia was losing her mind. The days passed where they each would touch her, give a hug good morning, or just give her a hug because they thought she needed it. It was so damn frustrating she held on to Cosivan a few seconds longer and even rubbed her breasts against his chest to try and get some sort of reaction. She felt like an absolute idiot. Maybe they really didn't feel the attraction she had for them.

This morning she was sitting next to Viktor on the couch and slowly eased her hand over his hand and he got all tense and then made an excuse to walk away. Following that Dusty was making a sandwich in the kitchen and he slid his hand along her waist and she pressed her ass back and felt his hard erection. He practically jumped to the other side of the table like she had a disease. She was so annoyed.

They were babying her one minute and then the next keeping their distance. She was getting antsy and when she opened the door to go outside a minute, two doors opened and Dusty and Viktor came out in a huff.

"What are you doing?" Viktor asked her in that tone of his. He had that little bit of Russian accent that came out when he was angry or on edge. She only recently picked up on it and she wondered if he usually hid it but was kind of off his game being stuck here like this.

"Getting some fresh air," she replied.

"Well, tell us first, and one of us can sit out here with you," Dusty added, crossing his arms in front of his chest and staring at her.

She exhaled in annoyance.

"When can we leave the house? You know, go for a walk, a ride, maybe a run?" she asked, feeling that loss of not being able to work out every day. She loved running and exercising, lifting weights and challenging her body. Doing the push-ups and sit-ups, even with the stitches aching, wasn't enough.

"There's a weight room down in the basement. Everything you need is in there. A treadmill, elliptical, a speed bike with the TV so you can participate in live spin classes," Dusty told her. She rolled her eyes at him.

They had all been being kind of testy with her lately. Since the other night when Aspen and her men came to visit. In fact, Aspen was supposed to negotiate a little shopping trip. She assured they would be safe and even suggested a disguise as precaution for Nalia. She smirked to herself. The men weren't too thrilled with that at all.

She felt their eyes on her and then realized she wasn't enjoying this. She felt caged in. She turned to look at Viktor and Dusty.

"There's nothing like running outdoors. Can't we do that? I mean do any of you work out?" she asked and then felt her cheeks warm as both very fit, muscular sexy men raised an eyebrow at her. "You know what I mean. Run?" she asked.

"No. No running," Dusty said. Now he was being firm and he was the quietest and calmest of the bunch.

She exhaled. "Why the hell not? We can pack guns and be ready just in case."

"The answer is no," Viktor stated firmly.

"Grrr." She growled and headed back inside.

She walked into the living room to see Cosivan and Chatham looking at some papers and at the laptop.

"What's going on?" she asked them.

"Nothing," Cosivan said and looked her over. She plopped down onto the couch.

"I want to go for a run."

"No," Chatham stated firmly.

"What? Why not?"

"Because Dusty and Viktor said no."

"I thought you were the boss of this thing. I need exercise. I'm going insane."

"The stitches. Remember," Chatham stated.

"The stitches, remember," she mimicked and then stood up and headed to her room.

She was in such a state and as she got to the top of the stairs there was Boian.

"Hey, what's going on?" he asked her and gave a small smile.

"Nothing. As usual. Can't do a damn thing. Can't go outside. Can't run. Can't deal with all your attitudes for no reason." She threw her hands up in the air.

"The stitches."

"Yeah, yeah, the stitches. Then take them out," she said and walked to her bedroom and slammed the door closed.

She felt so frustrated as she plopped down onto the bed and felt fine. She slid off of it and landed on the floor. Taking matters into her own hands, she began to do a bunch of push-ups then sit ups, letting off some steam. They were making her crazy. They were keeping their distance and being jail wardens. She practically threw herself at them one at a time and got no response but denial or they ran. What the hell? She growled some more until she exhausted herself and fell to the floor in a sweat.

"A shower. That's what I need, a nice cold shower."

* * * *

"She wants the stitches out. We can't keep this up," Boian said as he joined the others in the living room.

"We had to make sure that there really wasn't a suspicious sighting," Cosivan said to them.

"There wasn't. Storm confirmed that an hour ago," Dusty said.

"Well, every possible sighting needs to be investigated. We would do it ourselves but then showing our faces would surely indicate we have Nalia under our protection. We need to be diligent in protecting her," Cosivan told them.

"The closer we are to her the easier that would be. Protecting her, I mean," Chatham said.

"We discussed that for the last several nights," Cosivan replied.

"We're stalling. We want her, she wants us, let's claim her already," Viktor stated.

"You know I'm in," Boian replied.

"It needs to be done right. We need the right time and be sure about this," Cosivan said to them.

"We all want her. There's no right time but right away," Dusty said and they chuckled.

"Then the decision is final. There will be no going back, no regrets. We're willing to give up everything for Nalia. Everything," Cosivan said to the team.

"Yes," Boian said and the others agreed.

"We go slow. She's a virgin, as far as we know. It will take some time before we can take her three at a time. Got it?" Cosivan asked.

"Damn, I can't wait," Chatham said and rubbed his hands together.

"This is real. We're going to be a family. We're going to have Nalia to take care of and love," Dusty said.

"We're going to have our hands full," Viktor added.

"You have no idea," Boian said and Cosivan chuckled.

"Together. We'll take our time and make her ours, but we never let our guard down. I want two men always by the door keeping watch and ready."

* * * *

Nalia washed up and prepared for bed. She was looking into the mirror and lifted her white tank top to see how the stitches looked. She jumped when she heard the knock on the door.

"Yes," she said, and the door opened.

She turned and saw Boian standing there. He looked at her as she pushed the tank top down and then ran her fingers through her hair. She had to look away from him. She avoided their gazes because they were getting to her and the desire to have them, to feel them all touch her was becoming too difficult to ignore. She felt her heart racing every time they were near and it was getting annoying. Especially the fact that her nipples got all hard and her pussy actually leaked cream. From looking at them and being around them. Was that even normal?

She no longer cared that she wore the boy short panties and paraded around in her underwear in her room. They didn't seem to care or to show interest. It frustrated her. Sure, she was young, inexperienced, but damn it she was more than willing to allow them to teach her, to give her experience even if it meant breaking her heart and one day leaving her.

"I wanted to talk to you."

Like I care? I'm done with this. I can't take talking to you in my bedroom with you looking so sexy, so desirable and strong. God damn you, Boian. God damn all of you.

"Tomorrow. I'm tired," she said to him and then walked right past him. She stopped short when she saw Cosivan sitting on her bed. She noticed he had some items on the bed next to him. Scissors, ointment, and alcohol wipes.

"It's time to take those stitches out," Cosivan said to her, looking her over with those sultry, sexy, dark eyes of his.

I can't take this. I can't.

She licked her lower lip.

"Tomorrow would be fine," she said and stood still. Her heart was racing once again as that twinge of being disobedient and questioning Cosivan's order filled her gut. It was an order. Every word the man spoke was a command, a direction, an act of control, and damn it her pussy wept as usual. She shifted her weight and looked away from those commanding eyes. Cosivan's expression, as always so hard and firm and just plain angry, stared back at her. She felt that gut instinct and sense of intimidation. He was so big and powerful in every way.

"We do it now," he replied and his eyes roamed over her body and suddenly she wished she had more clothing on.

Boian reached for her, his hands landed on her hips and she gasped softly. Why did such a small touch turn her on so much? Why was she a glutton for punishment? These men didn't want her in the ways she wanted them. Hell, she was a virgin and more than willing to let them fuck her in every hole, use her to pass the time and take from her body just so she could feel some sort of connection. She needed them. They were already a part of her and they didn't want to have her be a part of them. *Fuck, I can't take it. I can't.* She planted her feet but Boian was so big, strong, and sexy, that when she felt his hard chest and even harder erection against her back and ass she stepped closer to Cosivan and the freaking bed.

When Cosivan opened his thighs for her to step between them she shivered from being this close to him. Thick wide shoulders like some football linebacker, and hard, thick, iron muscled thighs that immediately sent goose bumps over her skin as they touched her. She was much smaller than him, so as he glanced up at her, his face was in line with her breasts. She closed her eyes a moment and imagined him licking her nipple, maybe gripping her hips and thrusting his body against hers. She would come. Right here, standing between his legs if he showed even an ounce of desire like she had for him.

They were both silent. She felt his jean-covered thighs press against her bare skin. It made her body come alive. Was he doing this on purpose? Was he having fun teasing the wanton little virgin? Her anger boiled but one look into Cosivan's eyes and she knew to not ever challenge him or start a fight with him. But oh, how she wanted to and she didn't even know why. They made her crazy. Absolutely crazy. These were the only men, them and their team, that made her body react. It was wild.

"Your top," he said and then went to lift it higher but then Boian slipped his hands around her waist and slowly raised it. She stopped his hands from lifting it over her breasts. She glanced over her shoulder at him and he squinted at her as if questioning his control.

"No bra," she whispered.

She felt Cosivan's fingers against her skin on her belly nowhere near the stitches. They caressed over her firm abs and to her hips. He ran his hand along her boy shorts and she felt her pussy spasm.

Don't come, don't come, don't give in.

Then she heard the hardwood floor creak, and glanced up to see Viktor then Dusty and Chatham enter the room. Their shirts were undone, revealing all their sexy, muscular flesh and even some scars. Especially along Viktor's body.

She tightened her pussy.

They remained near the doorway and the wall but watched.

"These will come out nice and easy. Relax," Cosivan told her.

She snorted. *Yeah, right. Relax with five men half naked in my room looking like they want to taste me. Hell, I want to taste them. All of them.* She thought about lowering to her knees, pushing Cosivan down on the bed, and undoing his pants. She would whip out his cock and learn real fast how to please him with her mouth.

She felt her cheeks warm and knew a blush spread across her face.

She felt the tickle against her skin as Cosivan cut the first small stitch. She looked down and saw that there wasn't any scarring, just two small dots that already seemed to disappear. Cosivan's hands were so large against her body. She felt feminine, petite, and controllable. She would give him complete control of her body if he would accept her.

At the same time Boian kissed her bare shoulder and continued a path to her neck.

"Boian."

"Shhh. Not a word. No lies. Nothing but truth." He suckled against her skin. She shivered with desire.

What does he mean? Oh God, are they going to use me? Use my body? Yes. Oh yes, please let them. Let them take me. I don't care about tomorrow or next week or anything but feeling more and giving myself to them and remembering this moment together forever.

A second cut and the next stitch released. Cosivan's hands slid along her belly and then he cut the third stitch and she felt the tickle as he pulled them from her skin.

Boian ran his palm along the underside of her breast and as he moved it under her tank top she felt Cosivan's lips against her hip right where the stitches had been.

"So sweet and soft," Cosivan whispered, warm breath singing against her skin. She shivered again when he licked along her belly button and then over her tattoo.

When his teeth nipped her hipbone she thought her legs would give out.

She gasped and grabbed on to his shoulders.

Boian ran his hand under her hair to the base of her neck and gripped a handful of hair. She felt his control and her pussy actually spasmed.

"Isn't she beautiful?" he asked aloud. Her eyes popped open as she remembered the audience.

"What are you doing to me, Boian, Cosivan? What do you want?" she asked, her voice cracking.

"You," they said together and then Cosivan lowered to the floor, grabbed ahold of her hips and began kissing and licking her skin. He used his tongue and teeth to press down her bottoms as Boian lifted up her tank top to her neck, then covered her mouth and kissed her. She moaned and felt her pussy explode.

"Sweet mother, she's gorgeous," Chatham said and then she felt the others move closer but Boian was kissing her deeply. There were multiple hands touching her and then Cosivan was pushing down her panties, squeezing her ass, running a thick digit over the crack of her ass and she moaned.

She felt him lifting her thigh up over his shoulder. She pulled from Boian's mouth as Cosivan's mouth landed on her cunt. "Oh God. Oh!" she exclaimed.

"Easy, baby. Nice and slow, we want to explore you," Boian told her. Chatham licked along her nipple on one side while Dusty licked along the nipple on her other side. She gasped again as her pussy kept spasming.

She opened her eyes and tried to focus when she locked onto Viktor. He stood by the open door, arms crossed, gun on his hip. He held her gaze firmly.

"No more fighting and denying our feelings. Tonight we want to make you our woman," Viktor told her just as Cosivan suckled on her clit and tugged hard.

"Oh!" she moaned loudly.

She felt their hands lifting up her tank top then tossing it. Her large breasts bounced and then hands immediately cupped them. Dusty and Chatham. She locked gazes with them and saw the desire in their eyes and those hard, determined, challenging looks. She was in a heap of trouble. The good kind.

"You're perfect for us, Nalia. Perfect," Boian whispered against her ear. He pulled her hands from Cosivan's shoulders and kept her hands behind her back. She felt controlled, restrained with her breasts pushed forward, her pussy being feasted on with Cosivan's hard, experienced mouth and tongue, until Dusty licked her breast and tugged on her nipple. She moaned and Boian brought her hands lower behind her back and directly over his cock.

She shuddered and gasped, then felt her pussy gush cream.

"So fucking delicious. Damn, baby, I could eat your pussy all night," Cosivan said and she felt her mouth open in shock but then Boian pressed his hands over hers and made her stroke his cock. She followed his direction. Let him lead her because she had no clue at all. All this time she wished, she fantasized about making love to these men. Now here she was and they wanted her, and she didn't even know what to do or how it would feel.

Dusty cupped her cheeks and held her gaze. He was shirtless, and wearing only black boxer briefs. His jaw was firm, his dark brown eyes caring at the moment instead of angry as usual.

"Easy, baby. Let us guide you and we promise your first time, every time will be pleasurable." He kissed her lips and she kissed him back.

"Follow your gut, your heart," Boian said and she began to stroke his cock and then he released her hands and she continued to do it on her own while she kissed Dusty and let Cosivan have his way with her cunt.

She felt Boian's teeth graze along her side and to her other breast.

Just as she got used to Cosivan's tongue and teeth she felt him pull away and then thrust a finger up into her pussy. She rocked her hips and he eased it in and out until she got used to it. Then he added another one. When she felt him press his other finger over her anus and push inside of her at the same time she cried out, pulling from Dusty's mouth.

She felt sedated from his fingers and tongue and their combined ministrations. Never had she ever thought it would be like this or feel so amazing and perfect.

She grabbed on to Cosivan and pressed him back onto the bed. The move caused Boian to slide his cock against her anus and she shook but then covered Corsivan's mouth with hers. She tasted her scent on his lips and on his tongue and it did something to her. It made her feel wild, wanton and she thrust her hips as Boian played with her pussy and ass.

She could feel Dusty kissing her shoulder then down her back as Boian stroked a finger into her pussy from behind. He leaned closer and licked her cunt and then she felt Dusty's finger press over her anus.

"I love this ass. I've admired it for a long time and can't wait to fuck it," Dusty told her and pressed his finger deeper into her ass.

She moaned as she lifted her pelvis up and pressed her ass back.

Smack.

She pulled from Cosivan's mouth and nearly sprang up off of him. Cosivan gripped her tight. He drew her against his wide shoulders and forced her to keep kissing him. He tugged on her lips and then gripped her hair and held her close. He whispered against her lips.

"Let them explore you, too. You belong to us now and always." He plunged his tongue into her mouth and she held on to his chest as Dusty and Boian stroked her pussy and anus.

She was shaking and moaning when Cosivan pulled from her mouth.

"Condoms. Now," he ordered.

Fingers left her body and she almost cried out in anger. It had felt so good but then Cosivan rolled her to her back. He lifted up and pulled off his pants then lowered his mouth to her breasts. His heavy body nearly crushed her, his large hands gripping her dainty wrists as his mouth suckled her nipple hard. She moaned and leaked more cream. He was a wild lover. He was big, older, experienced and she felt fearful in a way of his capabilities and her lack of.

"Cosivan," she gasped and he lifted up and sat above her.

She glanced down and widened her eyes at the size of his cock. It was huge. It couldn't be a normal size for a man and she wondered how the hell it would fit into her. Suddenly she was more than just intimidated, she was downright panicked.

He cupped her cheeks and stroked a finger over her lips. She grabbed his wrist best she could with her fingers as he held her hands with one hand. He squinted at her. "Do you trust us?" he asked her.

She swallowed hard at his tone and the look in his eyes of determination, power, and control. "Yes."

"Good. I will fit because you were made for me and you were made for my team. Your body will adjust to our sizes and to our appetites. Do you want us as we want you?" he asked.

She thought about the fear, the reservations she had since she knew basically nothing about sex. Then she thought about how they each made her feel and how she wanted more of them. She couldn't seem weak or show the fear her inexperience brought out in her. These were grown men, American soldiers, Russian mobsters. They probably only had sex with women who knew how to please a man. She would have to learn how to please five of them and show them how capable and strong she was and how good she could be for them. She had to let go of the fear and just give in to the desire. She had nothing to lose. Nothing but her heart and her sanity.

She held his gaze as she parted her lips. He released her wrists and looked like he was retreating. She panicked. She needed to let him know she wanted this. She gripped his hand, brought his palm up her belly between her breasts and then tugged his finger into her mouth and suckled it. She felt sexy, wild, especially as those dark blue eyes turned almost animalistic. She was doing it to him. Driving him wild with desire. All his experience and lovers he had meant nothing. She felt that or at least wanted, needed to believe it as she gave him her virginity first.

"Nice and easy, lover," he whispered and like a pro he rolled a condom onto his very thick, hard cock and then spread her legs with his thighs.

"Tell me you're ready to become part of the team. To be mine?" he asked her very seriously.

"I want you. All of you."

He gave a very small indication of what had to be a smile for Cosivan before she felt his thick cock nudge at her entrance then pull back, teasing her.

"You're so wet, baby," he said to her as he used his thumb to test her pussy. He stroked it over her pussy lips then dipped it into her sopping wet cunt. She grabbed on to his wrist.

"Cosivan, please. I'm ready," she said to him. He eased down lower and wrapped her tight between his huge muscular arms and held her gaze as he slowly pushed his cock into her virgin pussy.

Inch by inch he eased into her as he kissed her lips, teased the corners of her mouth, and then pressed his tongue deeper as his cock nudged and nudged.

"So fucking tight. Let me in. Let me in," he demanded and she moaned as he pulled out, making her wonder if he changed his mind as the fear, the anger, the sadness consumed her and then he shoved all the way in, making her lose her breath and cry out.

"Cosivan!"

He held himself within her, letting her body adjust to the thick, foreign muscle nearly touching her womb. She sighed, realizing that she had done it. She finally lost her virginity and allowed a man that close to her.

"Mine," he whispered possessively against her neck and suckled her hard, making her forget about the pinch of pain and focus on the feel of being surrounded by Cosivan and made love to by her soldiers.

She rocked her hips as he lifted up and thrust back into her. She began to get the gist of it and welcome each thrust of his cock as it eased away this inner itch she had. She ran her fingers through his hair as he suckled her breast and feasted on her body.

She couldn't stop touching him. She loved the feel of hard, large muscles beneath her fingertips and then being able to run her fingers through his hair he always had so military perfect.

"Cosivan, oh, Cosivan," she moaned and tilted her head back as his hands manipulated her hips and roamed under her to her ass, spreading her ass cheeks, widening her thighs while he thrust balls deep. He was so big, so wild and practically crushed her and she loved it. Over and over again he stroked into her cunt until she was begging for mercy until another orgasm overtook all other emotions. He lifted up, pulled her legs higher against his sides, and chanted her name.

"Nalia! Nalia, my beautiful sexy Nalia," he said and then began to set a faster pace. Her breasts rocked and swayed, her pussy felt swollen and overwhelmed as he thrust and thrust and then she felt herself orgasm again as Cosivan came inside of her. He hugged her to him and rolled her to the side. He kissed her everywhere he could and she smiled, enjoying having sex for the very first time yet knowing it wasn't going to be the last.

He cupped her breast, leaned down, and licked the nipple. She stared at the ridges of all his muscles and the deep crevices of steel along his abs and thighs.

"Together. We need to take you one after the next so we are all your firsts." He kissed her before she could get her brain to respond. It made sense. But could she let all five men love her one after the next? The word *yes* exploded in her mind as Boian took Cosivan's position, rolling her to her back, spreading her thighs, then kissing her deeply as he pressed the tip of his cock to her very lubricated cunt.

* * * *

Boian's heart was racing. To hear Nalia's cries of passion made him nearly come as he watched. She was so giving and loving, plus looked small, feminine, and dainty under Cosivan as his leader was the first to take from her body and make her theirs.

Boian cupped her cheeks and eased his cock right into her cunt. "I can't wait. I can't not have you and make you mine, finally, baby." He covered her mouth and kissed her deeply. She ran her fingers along his ribs and hips then slid her hands over his ass as he deepened the strokes. He was on fire with love, pure love and even lust for this woman. She'd rocked his world several years before. Made him wish he could have chosen a different path yet knowing he never would have had the opportunity to meet her if it weren't for her father and for Viktor.

She kissed him back and he released her lips and shifted upward to look at her and see the passion in her eyes.

Her large breasts bounced up and down with every deep stroke. "I love your body, baby. You're so tight and perfect. We'll always protect you. With everything we have."

Her lips parted and her hands gripped his wrists as he thrust harder and faster into her cunt. "Mine. You're mine, baby."

"And you're mine, too," she said and he chuckled then lowered down to tug on her nipple, lick and suckle her breast then nip at it.

"Boian," she exclaimed and he smiled then leaned toward the other side and did the same thing. She grabbed on to his hair and head and brought him closer to her lips, kissing him deeply. He continued to stroke into her cunt and relish in the feel of knowing she was now part of him and belonged to him and his team. They would love her, cherish her, protect her, and make her feel like the most important woman in the world.

He thought about the danger she was in and about her abilities and how she survived and it made him fuck her faster, harder. He shifted his weight, pulled her thighs up high against his waist, and stroked until she cried out and he felt her inner muscles grip his cock like a vise.

"Oh fuck," he roared and came.

He kissed her everywhere and she ran her fingers through his hair and caressed his shoulders as he suckled her breasts then her neck until the bed dipped.

As he slowly released her nipple he looked to the right and there was Dusty stroking his cock and looking more than ready to claim their woman next.

One look at Nalia as she nibbled her bottom lip and he knew she wanted Dusty, too.

* * * *

Dusty took Nalia from Boian and pulled her on top of him. She straddled his waist and he smiled up at her, cupping her breasts.

"How are you feeling?" he whispered, using his thumbs to stroke both nipples. He felt her wet pussy over his belly.

"Incredible," she told him as she softly caressed his chest and ran her fingers gently over his nipples. She played with them softly until he pinched her nipples.

Her lips parted and their gazes locked. "Harder. Play with them harder, I like that," he said to her. She swallowed hard and looked incredible beautiful. She was their woman and no one else's. They were her firsts, her lasts, her everything.

She did as he said and she began to tug on his nipples. His cock hardened beneath her and she gasped. "So that's why you like it," she said to him and he heard the chuckles.

Her eyes widened and she looked behind him to his brothers.

She seemed embarrassed. He reached up and pulled her closer, her breasts now pressed against his chest.

"Oh baby, the things I'm going to teach you." He kissed her lips and then thrust his hips upward. He pulled back and she smiled softly.

"Like what, Dusty?" she asked.

He ran his hands along her ass and parted her cheeks.

"Like how to ride cock," he said and thrust up.

Her eyes widened and he couldn't help but feel dominant, excited, in complete control. She was so sexy he could come right here right now.

"I need inside of you, baby, or I'm going to spill my load right here. Please," he whispered and she lifted up and then reached between them without direction. She gripped his cock gently and then she eased her pussy down over it. Gripping his wrists, she closed her eyes. "Look at me," he demanded and she opened them and held on to his shoulders. "Ease that sweet, wet cunt over my cock. Lift up and down until you find a nice comfortable pace to ease that itch."

"Itch?" she asked as she lowered down and squinted. His cock was big and thick. All their cocks were and she was petite and they worried she may have difficulty at first. Then she parted her lips and breathed through the tightness. Before long she was moving up and down on his shaft and moaning as he played with her breasts then her ass.

"Ohh, that itch," she said, and he smiled as she rode him faster and faster.

He felt his cock grow thicker, harder and he knew he was going to come. She moaned loudly as the second set of hands landed on her and Chatham joined them.

Smack.

"Oh!" she cried out and came. Dusty felt her pussy leak all over his cock, lubricating her strokes. He gripped her hips and thrust upward as she thrust downward until they were both panting.

"Almost there. Fuck, I don't want to come."

Smack.

"Oh!" she cried out and he thrust up as he came and pulled her down and kissed her deeply.

They were trying to catch their breath when Chatham smacked her ass again and again.

"Chatham," she reprimanded and Dusty chuckled.

"He needs you, too," Dusty told her and kissed her lips as she sat up, smiling.

As he slid from her body Chatham lifted Nalia by her hips and placed her on all fours on the bed.

"Just like this, sexy mamma."

Dusty watched Chatham slide his palms along her thighs and her hips, spreading her legs. She gripped the comforter and looked forward right at Viktor, who waited patiently for his turn.

She licked her lips and Dusty chuckled then heard the series of smacks to her ass and the sound of her cries of pleasure fill the room.

* * * *

"Oh baby, you are in for it. Flaunting those sexy tits, teasing Viktor and me as we watched and waited."

He slid his fingers along her ass cheeks then dipped a digit into her pussy from behind. Nalia gripped the comforter and Chatham chuckled low. He used his other hand to massage her ass cheek then stroke cream from her pussy to her anus.

"So fucking tight. I like this little bud. Can't wait to fuck this bud."

"Oh God, Chatham, you're wild," she said, panting.

"You have no idea. But you will. Soon enough." He stroked the wet digit into her anus as he kept stroking his other finger into her pussy.

"Tell me you want me."

"I want you," she said immediately and he chuckled.

He pulled his finger from her ass and then the other digit from her pussy.

"Are you sure? You don't seem too sure," he teased her, bending over her body and suckling her neck.

She shivered beneath him. "I'm sure. I'm very, very sure." The others chuckled and he smiled against her neck.

"I expect a lot from you, Nalia. A real lot," he said, sliding his palm along her ass then pulling back and smacking her ass cheek.

She jerked forward. "Oh God," she moaned and he could see the cream drip between her legs.

"Someone likes getting spanked. I think this is going to be a nice form of discipline for our woman. Don't you think so, Viktor?" he asked.

She lifted her head up and Viktor stared at her, arms crossed and looking serious.

"Definitely," he said firmly and Chatham chuckled.

He pulled her hips back, aligned his cock with her pussy, and then massaged her shoulders. "This is a very fine body you have, Nalia. Very fine indeed. But can you handle five lovers? Can you handle a cock in your mouth, one in your tight little pussy and one in this sexy, round, tight ass?" he asked.

Smack.

"Oh God, yes. Yes, I want to. I want you to do whatever you want to me. I need you."

His eyes widened and his heart soared with pleasure and adoration. He saw his brothers' expressions and then watched as Viktor began to undress and Dusty took his position at the door to guard it.

"Fuck yeah. You're ours and we will possess every inch of you. Every, fucking, inch," he said firmly as he inched his cock into her pussy and she shoved back onto it, shocking him.

Smack, smack, smack.

"Oh."

"Watch it, Nalia. I could have hurt you."

"Never. Never would happen. Give it to me. I need you and then I want Viktor. I want all of you over and over again." She carried on and he lost it. She was so giving, so loving and wild that he began to fuck her from behind and thrust and stroke until his legs ached and his heart felt like it might burst from his chest. He gripped her hips and pounded away until he found his release and came just as Nalia did.

They both moaned and came together then he hugged her from behind.

Viktor was there standing in front of the bed, watching them.

"Nalia," he said firmly and Chatham caressed her ass and hips as he kissed her shoulders then eased out of her cunt. She gasped and then nearly fell to the bed.

"Come here," Viktor said firmly.

One glance around the room as the others watched and he knew this was perfect. He knew they made the right decision and that this moment, this night would bind them even greater and stronger than all those years in the service ever could have. All because of Nalia.

* * * *

Nalia was determined to make love to all five men. She wanted to be strong for them and capable for them even though her pussy ached and her body felt sore already. One look at Viktor and that firm jaw, those large muscles and blond hair, and she was wet all over again.

He stood by the edge of the bed and she sat up with her hands on her thighs, her legs tucked underneath her.

"Open for me," he said firmly.

She felt her heart pounding inside of her chest. She could do this.

"Are you sore?" he asked her.

In her mind she debated about telling him she was but then he might wait to make love to her and she really wanted them all together so they each took her virginity or at least felt they had. She eased her fingers along her groin, saw his cheeks cave in like he was biting the inside of them and she pressed fingers to her cunt. She circled her labia, then stroked into her pussy. She saw his eyes widen and squint at her as the others made mumbled noises.

"Not sore, but very, very wet."

He moved closer to her and held her gaze as he bent down slightly. He moved his fingers to her cunt and checked for himself. She gasped and parted her lips, feeling the cream drip down her ass. "Put a condom on me," he said to her and dropped one onto the bed as he continued to stroke her cunt as she sat there, legs wide open. She felt like she could fall back and off balance with every thrust of his fingers but she was determined to show him she could handle each of their personalities. She opened the packet and he gave her directions.

"Do we need these? Is it because you're so experienced with women?" she asked him.

His eyes widened. "For your protection," he said to her.

"Mine? But I have an IUD," she told him and he pulled the condom from her hands and lowered her to her back. He spread her legs as she heard the others make comments and talk about not knowing that and Viktor grabbed her hips and lowered over her. "Nothing ever between us. Ever," he said and stroked into her in one deep thrust.

She smiled to herself. She had a feeling they didn't know but thought because they probably had sex all the time they were protecting her by wearing condoms. Seemed she was wrong, yet did something right because Viktor had to take her last and he wound up taking her with no barriers whatsoever.

She hugged his shoulders best she could as he thrust into her pussy. He rocked into her so hard the bed groaned. "You're so beautiful," she told him as she ran her palms along his cheeks and then her fingers through his hair.

"No, baby, you're beautiful. You're everything," he said to her and then began to feast on her breasts as he thrust slower into her pussy.

She tilted her head back and moaned as tiny vibrations had her coming in spurts of pleasure. He lifted up and gripped her hips again then pulled her thighs higher against his waist.

"You feel so hot and tight. Your pussy is gripping my cock and I can hardly move. Damn, baby, you're amazing and now you're mine." He lowered down and thrust faster and faster into her. She countered his thrusts best she could until her thighs began to ache and finally her body gave out. It was too much. Felt too good and she cried out her release as Viktor moaned then came inside of her. He kissed her on the mouth and then all over her body as he caressed her skin. She could barely keep her eyes open and she didn't want to. She wanted to keep them closed and just absorb every moment and every lover she had tonight. They were hers and she was theirs. Always and forever.

* * * *

Viktor squeezed Nalia to him as she moaned in her sleep. She was breathing heavy like she was in a panic.

"What's wrong?" Cosivan asked and he caressed her shoulder.

"A bad dream," Viktor whispered and they both caressed her body. Nalia jerked upright and then gasped.

"It's okay. You're safe and you're okay," Viktor told her, cupping her cheek. The bedroom door opened and Boian, Chatham, and Dusty walked into the room. It was early morning and they were dressed.

Viktor saw the fear in her eyes and the tears roll down her cheeks. She seemed to realize she was safe and with them and then pulled the covers up to cover her body but Cosivan was pressing them down.

He cupped her breast and she jerked to the right to look at him. "You're ours. It wasn't a dream. You belong to us now and we belong to you."

She swallowed hard and then wrapped her arms around his shoulders and hugged him tight. Cosivan rolled to his back, taking her with him and he locked gazes with Viktor, a concerned expression on his face.

Viktor caressed her back and then her bare ass. He gazed at the others. "Is she okay?" Chatham asked.

"She's fine. We'll take care of her and bring her down for breakfast," Cosivan said, his tone tight, hard as always.

She lifted up and kissed Cosivan and when she moved she moaned.

"Are you sore?" Cosivan asked.

She shook her head and lowered down to kiss him. Viktor kissed along her shoulder then to her ass. She widened her thighs and lifted up as Cosivan cupped her breasts and began to feast on them.

"You sure you feel okay, baby?" Viktor asked as he caressed her hair from her shoulder and continued to massage her ass.

"Yes," she told him.

Cosivan gave her hips a hard shake, and she gasped and looked down at him. He released a nipple but kept his mouth close. "Truth," he demanded. Then suckled her breast again.

"A little," she admitted.

They had washed her up as she slept last night and were sure to apply some lotion to her body. A glance at the nightstand and Viktor saw the new bottle of lube by the bedside table.

"Maybe you need a little rest," Cosivan whispered to her.

She shook her head.

"I want you again. No barriers. I want you to have all of me. I don't want to stop feeling safe and connected. Does that scare you?" she asked Cosivan.

He gripped her hips and moved her with him to the side of the bed. Viktor got up and moved in behind her.

Cosivan gripped her cheek and neck as she straddled his hips.

"Nothing scares me," he told her and then she lifted up and she slowly sank down on Cosivan's cock.

Cosivan gripped her hips and spoke to her in Russian. He told her how beautiful she was and how he would never leave her side and always protect her.

"I don't know what you just said, but don't stop, Cosivan. I love how it sounds," she told him and Viktor chuckled. He started to kiss her back as he stood behind her. He gripped her hips and moved her up and down, assisting with her strokes on top of Cosivan.

"More, Viktor," she said to him. He stroked a finger along her ass and then parted her ass cheeks. He could smell her perfume combined with soap from last night. Leaning forward, he nipped at her ass cheeks one after the next and she shuddered then moaned.

When he stuck his tongue out and began to lick her anus she moaned some more.

"Ahhh, I love the sound you coming, baby. I love that look in your eyes and how giving you are," Cosivan said and he cupped her cheek and kissed her lips. Viktor stared at her body and caressed it then pressed his finger into her ass. She was wet and aroused.

"Viktor. Oh God, it burns."

"Easy, baby, let him get that ass ready. Viktor and I are going to take you together," Cosivan said and she shivered and then nodded her head. "Good girl. Relax and let him in," Cosivan told her then thrust upward, making her gasp. She held on to his shoulders and Viktor went to reach for the lube but couldn't reach it with his finger in her ass.

"Here." Boian entered the room wearing only his boxers now as he grabbed the lube and passed it to Viktor.

Viktor nodded. "Joining us, brother?" he asked him.

"Fuck yeah," Boian said.

Nalia moaned again as Boian caressed along her shoulder to her hair. She looked at him just as Viktor pressed lube to her ass.

"Oh God," she moaned.

Boian cupped her cheeks then leaned down and kissed her. "You're so beautiful. So giving," he said when he released her lips. Viktor pressed in and out of her ass as Cosivan thrust upward into her cunt.

"Together. We want you," Boian said.

"I'll try," she whispered and Cosivan gripped her arms and pulled her lower so they were chest to chest. He widened his thighs and spread her open as Viktor thrust two fingers into her ass.

"She's ready," Boian said, caressing her hair and using his other hand to caress his cock.

"Boian, oh God, please. Show me. Show me how to please all of you," she said and then licked Cosivan's nipple.

"Fuck. Get into her ass now, Viktor," he ordered.

Viktor chuckled. He'd never seen their leader so on edge and out of control before. It was amazing to witness and to know little ol' Nalia did it to him. Hell, she did it to all of them.

Cosivan spread his thighs and Viktor pulled his fingers from her ass. "Here I come, love. Let me in," he told her. She exhaled and he slowly pressed his cock into her ass. He nudged and nudged when he heard the floor creak and saw Chatham and Dusty standing there. He gave a wink and then he stroked a little deeper, pulled back, and then sank all the way in. He, Cosivan and Nalia all moaned.

"Holy fuck, that's hot," Chatham said and Nalia moaned louder as she raised up. Boian cupped her cheek as he stood by the side of them and brought his cock to her mouth. "Want to taste me?" he asked her.

"Yes," she said and lowered down as if she couldn't wait and didn't need to be asked again if she wanted it. She twirled her tongue over the base then licked and suckled him into her mouth.

"Sweet mother, I love this mouth. Fuck yeah, baby," Boian grunted.

Viktor tensed up. "I can't move, she's so fucking tight. I'm already fucking there," he said.

Cosivan chuckled. "Me too. Holy fuck."

They all began to move into her and Nalia kept up. She was moaning and they were grunting when Viktor felt his body convulse then come, shooting his seed into her ass. He eased out slowly and Boian came next, but she didn't release him, she kept sucking his cock until he grabbed her hair and grunted. "Nalia, oh God," he said and she released him and he fell back but Dusty caught him, laughing.

"Did I do something wrong?" she asked.

"No. More than right. You're perfect," Cosivan said as he rolled her to her back and thrust into her fast and deep until she cried out again and he found his release. She hugged Cosivan to her and Viktor smiled at Boian and the others. The sight of Nalia crushed under Cosivan was arousing, and she didn't complain. Instead she held him to her and Cosivan worried about his weight but she fought him on it, clinging to him like a monkey even when he lifted her up with ease and rolled to his side. He gave her ass a slap. She gasped and then he pulled her close and kissed her forehead where they cuddled until Chatham and Dusty wanted their turn to love her together.

* * * *

"Now the three of you can make breakfast," Chatham said, taking Nalia from Cosivan and lifting her up into his arms. She straddled his waist and ran her fingers through his hair.

"Good morning, *Printessa*," Chatham said to her, calling her Princess. Her eyes sparkled and he felt it in his heart. He kissed her deeply then hugged her to him, walking her into the bathroom.

Dusty started up the water in the large walk-in shower. Chatham handed her to Dusty, who kissed her softly on the lips then set her feet down.

"We're going to take good care of you, *sladkaya*. Our little sweetie," Dusty said then kissed her softly before he grabbed the soap and began to wash her up.

"Arms up," Dusty ordered and she did immediately. Chatham watched her as she closed her eyes and let Dusty lather soap along her body. He moved in behind her and massaged her breasts then nipped her shoulder. She looked incredible, like some goddess as the suds dripped from her large breasts and she stood between them. She was petite, feminine, and sexy. He couldn't resist reaching out to help massage the shampoo into her long blonde hair. Dusty turned her to face the water and to face him. As he helped add conditioner then rinse it, Nalia reached for Dusty's cock.

"Nalia, your hands feel so good," he said to her, leaning back against the wall. Chatham caressed her shoulders then ran his hands along her waist, pulling her back. She knew what he wanted and she immediately lowered down and began to suck on Dusty's cock.

The sight of Dusty's hands gripping her wet hair as the water flowed over her body was erotic and wild. Chatham slid his fingers along the crack of her ass to her pussy and pressed into her.

She moaned softly.

"Someone is very, very wet," he said to her and then locked gazes with Dusty.

"I think she was made for Team 13," Dusty said then clenched his teeth.

"This body was made for all of us," Chatham told her. He spread her thighs, making her bend into a wider stance and he continued to stroke her pussy. He stared at her round ass, and massaged the globes with one hand while fingering her cunt with the other. "I can't resist, she looks edible," he said and Chatham lowered down and licked her anus back and forth. She moaned and shook as she came from his ministrations and he used the cream to coat her anus.

"I need you. I want this ass, Nalia," he said to her and she continued to suck Dusty faster but gave her response by pushing her ass against his fingers.

He chuckled.

"Here I come," he said and removed his fingers then slowly slid his cock back and forth against her pussy and her rectum. She wiggled her ass and Dusty gave it a slap from above. Chatham looked up to lock gazes with Dusty, who was smiling wide.

"Together," he whispered and Chatham nodded.

He slid his cock into her ass slowly. It took several nudges since she was tight and small but finally he slid all the way in and moaned against her.

She pushed her ass back and Dusty gripped her hair.

"I want to be inside of you when I come, slow down, *Milaya*," Dusty said, calling her his sweetheart.

The water continued to fall between them and add to the erotic feel of the moment. Chatham could hardy stroke into her ass it was so tight and his cock so thick and hard. He knew it was only a matter of strokes before he came.

"Nalia. Oh God, Nalia, your ass feels incredible. Fucking incredible." He grunted then began to move faster and faster. She pulled from Dusty's cock and slid her fingers into her cunt as she grabbed on to Dusty.

"Holy fuck, Chatham, she's fingering her cunt," he informed him and Chatham lost it. He thrust into her three more times then came.

He slid his fingers over her pussy and moved her fingers away. He stroked her cunt and she moaned and begged for more.

"Oh please. Please, I'm so swollen," she said to them.

"Maybe Dusty can help you," he said to his brother then lipped an apology for not taking her together. Dusty chuckled and as Chatham pulled from her ass Dusty lifted her up, pulled her into his arms, and kissed her.

He pressed her against the wall, aligned his cock with her pussy, and shoved into her.

"Oh!" she exclaimed and gripped his shoulders then began to kiss Dusty all over his face, his neck, everywhere.

Chatham watched as Dusty rocked his hips at record speed, talking to her in Russian, telling her she was his everything and the sexiest, most amazing woman he ever fucked. Thank God Nalia didn't understand Russian or she might take offense to a comparison, but that's how fucking incredible she was and how wild she made them.

* * * *

Dusty couldn't get enough of her. She was so giving, so strong and passionate he felt unworthy of someone so precious and beautiful inside and out. He was crazed, feeling wild and animalistic as he suddenly wanted in every hole, claiming her his woman. She gripped him tighter and he saw her eyes glaze over then she exploded in orgasm. He licked her lips and eased a finger into her ass. She was slick and wet.

"I want to fuck this ass, baby. I got to fuck this mouth, this pussy but I need your ass."

"Yes, do it, Dusty, take me," she told him, panting.

He tilted back, pulling from her pussy and aligned his cock with her anus. The water cascaded over them and he held her gaze as he slid his thumb against her pussy lips. "Sexy, sweet, and all mine," he said then eased his cock into her ass. She wiggled and lowered, wanting him inside of her, too. He reached out and thumbed her breast, pinched the nipples and tugged hard as he stroked all the way into her ass.

"Oh God, you're so big. Oh," she moaned.

That was it. Enough taking time and enough games. He began to stroke faster, deeper into her ass and watched her beautiful breasts bounce and sway.

"You're perfect, Nalia. So sexy and giving. Your ass is fucking tight as hell. I won't last long," he told her and stroked in and out of her. She slid her fingers lower and pressed them to her pussy and that was it.

"Fuck," he said aloud then thrust and thrust until he came, shouting her name and filling her ass with his seed. It was carnal and wild but made him feel content in ownership and love. The word popped into Dusty's head and he was shocked but pleasantly accepting to the fact he loved her. He never loved a woman before. Didn't think he was capable of it, until now.

He slid from her ass and held her close then kissed her. She ran her fingers all over him, squeezing, massaging his muscles, and showing her love for him as well.

"To many other mornings just like this one, Printessa." He kissed her forehead before he hugged her close and smiled wide.

Chapter 6

Boian watched Nalia as she tried to run from Dusty and beat him to the house. They just got back from a run, something they all enjoyed doing with her almost every day. She was pumping her arms and trying to beat him when Dusty snagged her around the waist and hoisted her over his shoulder. Her laughter then scolding could be seen and heard from where he stood watching.

Boian chuckled and shook his head as he watched Dusty run his hands along her ass and right under her shorts. She reached back and slapped his hand.

"Oh, there'll be none of that. I own this ass," Dusty said and gave it a slap.

"Have a nice run?" he asked as they approached the stairs. Dusty set her feet down saying yes, they did have a good run, but Nalia said no, then took the bottle of water and took a sip.

"We did, too," Dusty stated. She gave him a mean expression.

"You cheat. I was beating you," she added.

Dusty ran his hand along her hip then gave her ass a slap. "Not a chance," he said.

She stepped back and placed her one hand on her hip while holding the water bottle.

"You're being a chauvinist," she told him firmly.

Boian smirked as Dusty looked over her body and the tight tank top that hit mid belly, showing off her sexy abs and the short spandex shorts that were tight and hugged her figure.

"No, baby, I think it's cute you trying to beat me, but a man is made differently than a woman. It will never happen," he said, licking his lips.

Boian knew that Dusty was teasing her, but she didn't realize that, and the next thing he knew, she was making her anger known. She stepped closer to Dusty and ran one hand up his chest under his shirt.

"You're right, we are made so differently." She pressed her hand lower then eased over his crotch as she spoke. "Men think with their cocks, women use their heads." She poured the bottle of water over Dusty's head.

"Nalia!" he roared and she ran behind Boian before Dusty could grab her.

"Let me at her. She's going to have a nice pink ass in about ten seconds," he said, trying to get past Boian.

Boian was laughing.

"I think you're even, Dusty."

Dusty stopped and stared at Boian. "Even? How the fuck so?"

"You insulted her. She didn't know you were teasing."

Nalia took off into the house and Boian laughed.

Dusty ran his fingers through his wet hair and then started chuckling.

"She is something else. Totally caught me off guard," Dusty admitted.

"Looked like she almost beat you," Boian added.

"She came pretty fucking close," he admitted and then shook his head. "What are we going to do? We can't live out here forever."

"I don't know. I think I could get used to this," Boian stated.

Dusty looked at him with a serious expression. "We have businesses to take care of and responsibilities. Decisions are going to have to be made."

"I know. Cosivan is in contact with Nicolai. I think we may have to head back to Chicago, or at least a few of us. Perhaps staying there a few weeks at a time for now until Vincent is located and taken care of."

"Vincent isn't our only problem," Cosivan said, interrupting them. Boian squinted his eyes at him. Cosivan seemed angry.

"Looks like Scarlapetti is still running his business and has some supporters. Nicolai believes he knows what they're after and unfortunately it involves all of us and real estate we own with Nicolai. Romeo Lapella has been sneaking in some people to steal shit right under Nicolai's nose. With us being away the past few months, things appear like we're giving up control. We have to head back."

"But Nalia," Boian started.

"I know. She isn't going to be happy about this, but for the time being we will take turns showing face in Chicago and do our best to maintain control of our investments with Nicolai. He assigned some of our friends but it isn't like when we show face," Cosivan said to them.

"When do we leave and who goes first?" Boian asked.

"I'll go and stay as long as needed. If I need help I'll send for one of you next."

"Cosivan, this is a shared responsibility. Nalia is now part of our family and our personal responsibility. If she's going to be involved with us then she's involved with this. We need to sit her down and explain," Boian said.

Dusty agreed.

"Tonight. We'll talk to her about it tonight, and then I'll leave for Chicago in the morning," Cosivan told them.

Boian felt his heartache and heaviness consume him. He was worried to say the least. It was different to be worried about his team members, his brothers, but now they had a woman, they had Nalia and she may not be able to accept this part of their lives. He didn't want to leave her again. It reminded him of the past and how Karlicov forbade him to ever see her again, and now he was in love with her.

That was another issue they needed to face. Telling Karlicov and Nicolai that they claimed Nalia as their woman, that they were now her protectors and hopefully, one day, her husbands.

* * * *

Nalia jumped the second she felt the arm wrap around her waist from behind. How the hell did they do that? Sneak up on her even in the shower?

"You got away without receiving your punishment," Dusty whispered against her ear and then rocked his hips against her ass. She felt his palm slide along her ass and she stuck it out, anticipating the smack.

"You didn't catch me," she replied, teasing him.

Smack.

She gasped as the sting aroused her, the water adding to the effect.

"Lucky for you, I'm a forgiving person," he said and moved that same hand along her hip down to her pussy. He cupped her mound and used his thigh to part her legs.

"Open for me, *Milaya*," he said and suckled her neck as she parted her thighs and felt his fingers stroke up into her cunt.

Her lips parted and water cascaded over them. She felt his cock against her ass and she craved it. She loved when her men were deep inside of her.

"What does that mean, Dusty?" she asked him.

He pressed her hair to the side with his free hand and suckled her neck and collarbone then trailed kisses along her shoulders. He cupped her breast and plunged his fingers in and out of her cunt.

"*Milaya?*" he asked then lowered, letting his cock press between her legs to where his fingers pumped and then her ass.

"Yes," she moaned.

He pulled his fingers from her mound and replaced them with his cock. He gripped her hips, and bent to align his cock with her pussy and slowly sank into her pussy. "Sweetheart, darling, that's what it means," he said and exhaled. She relaxed and moaned softly along with him, feeling full, complete now that they were so deeply connected.

He began to rock into her cunt and she lowered a little further. He grabbed her arms and pressed her palms to the wall then ran his palms along her arms to her back then her hips and ass. He pounded into her from behind. "So fucking sexy. I love this body Nalia. I love it," he told her and then leaned closer over her and slowed his strokes. He took his time, and clasped his fingers through hers against the wall. She felt the difference in him. He was loving her, deepening the connection and taking his time. She felt him suckle her skin against her neck and then he said things to her in Russian she didn't understand, yet felt in her heart.

"Dusty," she moaned and then tightened as she felt his cock grow thicker, harder.

"Mine. Always," he said and she felt her core tighten and then the orgasm hit her. Dusty came next, rocking his hips and thrusting into her three more times.

* * * *

"We have another situation on our hands," Chatham told Boian and Dusty. Cosivan stood there with his arms crossed. He already knew the bad news.

"What is it now?" Boian asked.

Chatham exhaled.

"We lost Cobra and Zinc."

"What?" Dusty asked.

"They were taken out at the club on Fuller Street. It was made to look like a carjacking but both got a bullet to the back of the head," Chatham said to them.

"This is bullshit. Was it Scarlapetti's men?" Viktor asked.

Viktor knew he would take it the hardest. Zinc and he did their basic training and then Special Forces training together. When Zinc got out of the service he had a little sister, Nina, who was on her own, practically living on the streets, a fucked up knee and was suicidal. Viktor got him the help he needed, assisted in getting Zinc and Nina a place to live, help her go to college, work at the club as a manager, and then hired Zinc as one of their security guys for the club they owned and operated on Fuller Street. This was another direct hit against the Merkovicz family.

"What about Nina? Who is with her and taking care of her?" Viktor asked.

"Right now she's at Nicolai's home and under the security detail. Our sources believe this hit was from Lapella. We're now dealing with two asshole Mafiosos who seek revenge against Nicolai and Karlicov," Chatham said to him.

"I'm going to have to go with Cosivan. Zinc would expect me to watch over her and protect her."

"We're going to have to go back as we discussed," Cosivan added.

"What's going on?"

They all turned to see Nalia standing there in a short blue sundress, barefoot and appearing upset.

"Who is Nina?" she asked and looked directly at Viktor.

"We were going to discuss this with you later tonight, but it seems we need to talk about things now. We'll have to head out in the next couple of hours," Cosivan told her.

"Head out? Where? You're leaving me?" she asked, suddenly looking scared.

Cosivan walked over to her and took her hand. "Some things have happened back in Chicago. These men, the ones who went after your father, are going after our clubs and just killed two of our friends," he told her.

"You can't go. What if they try to kill you?" she asked.

Chatham approached. He caressed her cheek and looked down into her dark blue eyes. He could see her fear. He felt it, too. "We have no choice and this is what we do, Nalia. As our woman, you need to accept our responsibilities and not ask questions," Chatham told her and her eyes widened.

"It's the way it has to be," Cosivan said and she swallowed hard then looked toward Viktor then back at Cosivan.

"When will you leave and how long will you be gone?" she asked Cosivan.

"In a few hours and we don't know yet. We'll work it out, it's nothing for you to worry about," Cosivan said to her.

"Nothing for me to worry about? I do worry. I will worry a lot, because that's what people do when they care."

"Nalia, don't give us a hard time about this. It's the life you will have now. Our positions involve danger and we need to go in order to keep protecting you. Now I don't want to hear another word. Accept it," Cosivan stated firmly.

Nalia swallowed and then pulled away from him and walked away. Cosivan ran his fingers through his hair and headed toward the desk.

"I'll make the arrangements," he stated firmly.

"You could have been a little calmer with her. She doesn't understand," Boian said to him.

Viktor placed his hands on his hips. "She needs to learn fast," he added.

"She's a smart woman. She'll get over it and learn quickly. Viktor, let's get the flight arrangements ready and plan to leave in a few hours," Cosivan said straight faced but Chatham had a feeling leaving Nalia was getting to him as well.

"We'll make the arrangements. You two should spend some alone time with Nalia to ease her mind. Who knows how long it will be before you can head back here," Dusty said to them.

Cosivan looked at Viktor. "You go, I'll be there shortly."

* * * *

Nalia stood by the window in the bedroom looking out toward the fields. It was so green and lush out there. The property was amazing and the trails through the wooded areas so much fun to run through and explore. She loved it out here, and that surprised her because she really saw herself as a city girl. She enjoyed the hustle and bustle of it all and the business, corporate world she had a taste of the last few years.

Her heart was pounding inside of her chest. She felt conflicted inside. Like she shouldn't be angry, sad, worried about her men because they expected her to be a brave, supportive soldier. But she was human, and she was so empty inside before they became part of her. It was frustrating to learn about each man's personalities and then to understand what they expected from her. She didn't know what to do, but just saying, "Okay, whatever you say, honey" was not her personality or her instinctual reaction to them heading directly into danger. So what that they were some sort of heavies for the Russian mob. They were her lovers, her men, her family and she wanted to protect them as much as they wanted to protect her.

"Nalia."

She jumped when she heard her name. She turned to see Viktor standing there. God, he was so gorgeous. He looked hot in his dark jeans and white button down shirt. His blond hair was slicked back perfect as usual, and those blue eyes and playboy smile made her thighs quiver with desire.

"I know you're upset and worried. It's all new to us. This relationship and having you to worry about and protect. You need to understand our positions and maybe this is partially our faults because we haven't sat down and explained what we do."

She shook her head. "You don't need to explain. I need to accept this, but it isn't easy. I was all alone, and lost so much and felt like I didn't know what I had left, if anything or anyone, to even care. But I took a chance on the five of you and gave you all of me. It just hurts to see how easily Cosivan, the rest of you can just not feel anything, or struggle to leave me, too."

She looked away and he was in front of her fast. He pulled her into his arms and held her close. "Are you out of your mind? Of course we don't want to leave you and this is a great struggle, but our friends, our family need us, too. These men are trying to destroy what we've all worked hard for. They killed two great men and one of them, Zinc, was a close friend of mine."

He pulled her over to the bed and sat down. He lifted her up and she straddled his waist as she held on to his shoulders. Viktor caressed up her thighs and under the skirt.

"Zinc and I went through basic training and then Special Forces training together. We went through heavy shit in our lives, and when Zinc returned from serving he was not the same man. He was suicidal, angry and had no one but a little sister who needed taking care of. She practically lived on the streets. I had to help him find her because he was so screwed up she disappeared on him. Then all they had were each other, so I helped them."

"Is that Nina?" she asked and he nodded his head.

"She's been working for us, we've helped her through college, and now her only family, her brother, is dead. Cosivan was planning on heading back to try and show face and bump up security and do what needed to be done. Now that this happened, I need to go with him so I can assign men to watch over Nina and take the precautions we need to take to ensure no one else gets killed. Without going into details, we have to stop this shit."

She felt the tears reach her eyes. She knew what it was like to feel all alone and to think her father, her only relative left, was dead. Nina really had no one but them.

"Nina needs you. She won't trust anyone but you probably. I understand. I'll worry about you and Cosivan."

He gave her a soft smile and reached up to cup her cheek.

"I'll think of you while I'm gone. I know it's going to be hell." He covered her lips and kissed her. She held on to his shoulders and kissed him back, knowing she would miss him terribly. That kiss grew deeper and soon he was caressing his palms along her ass and under her dress then pulling from her lips and lifting it up over her head. Her breasts bounced and he tossed the dress, then cupped her breast and suckled on the tiny bud. She ran her fingers through his hair and then over her shoulders, down his arms, as she lifted up, manipulating his jeans to undo the button and undress him.

He released her breast and she moaned as she held his gaze. "I need you."

"I need you, too," she replied.

"So do I."

She heard Cosivan's voice and gasped as she turned toward the doorway. He was pulling off his shirt and undoing his jeans as Viktor got undressed.

Cosivan stalked toward her, looking her body over then hoisting her up against him to kiss her deeply. She straddled his waist and kissed him back, ran her fingers through his hair and ravaged him, not caring about earlier and his hard knock ways.

She felt him shoving his pants down and stepping from them then he ran his hands along her ass and stroked her crack. He pulled from her mouth.

"My turn to fuck this ass and make you think about us when we're not here and we're in Chicago working."

Her body shivered and both her ass and her pussy seemed to react to his tone and his words.

"Climb up onto Viktor and ride him, while I grab the lube."

He lowered her over Viktor, who lifted her up high. She gasped when she felt the smack to her ass from Cosivan and then Viktor lowered her pussy right over his face, making her lose her balance and grab on to the comforter behind his head.

"Oh Viktor. Oh God," she moaned as he suckled on her clit hard and Cosivan chuckled.

She began to rock her hips when she felt Cosivan's hands massaging her shoulders then cupping her breasts. He ran his large hands from her nipples, tugging and pulling them, massaging them, down to her ribs and behind her to her ass.

"Time to share, Viktor," he ordered and Viktor lifted her up only for Cosivan to take her hips and pull her down over Viktor's cock. She reached underneath her to assist and then felt the thick muscle as it stretched her pussy and she sank down upon him.

Just as she lifted up and lowered back down, Cosivan caressed against her back and pressed lube to her ass. She tightened up.

"Oh no, baby, don't even think about it. I got a nice big, thick cock that's going to fuck this sexy ass good. You relax those muscles so I don't hurt you. I want you feeling nothing but pleasure," Cosivan said in that deep, hard tone of his. She felt her pussy spasm and then Viktor chuckled as he thrust upward.

"I think she likes being ordered around, Cosivan." Viktor continued to thrust upward.

Cosivan stroked her ass, adding another finger. "I think so, too," he said and then smacked her ass cheek on the right side, massaged it and then smacked the left side and massaged it. He gave her ass a squeeze. "I can't wait. Fuck," he said and pulled his fingers from her ass then spread her thighs a little wider, making her press her chest closer against Viktor. They maneuvered her back further and now her ass was hanging over the side of the bed and it felt like Viktor's hips were on the edge, too.

"I need room. I'm a big fucking man," Cosivan whispered and leaned down to suckle her neck.

"Oh God, Cosivan. Oh," she moaned. The anticipation was killing her. She felt the tip of Cosivan's cock at her anus. He slid it back and forth, pressed just the tip in, and then pulled out. Her belly quivered and she felt the chills, the desire to feel his cock in her ass. She pushed back.

"Please, Cosivan."

He suckled harder. "You want this cock in you now, Nalia?" he whispered against her ear then pressed the thick, hard tip in.

"Yes, Cosivan. Yes," she begged.

Viktor cupped her breasts and squeezed them. "I need a taste, lower down," he ordered and she lowered down to let Viktor suckle her breast and at the same time Cosivan spread her ass cheeks and his large hands held on to her hips and he stroked slowly into her ass.

He was huge. So damn big she felt her muscles stretching to accommodate him and she panicked. "Let me in," he grunted and she looked at Viktor.

"You look so fucking incredible right now. As soon as he's in that sexy ass, we're going to fuck you long and hard just the way you like it, baby," Viktor encouraged her then kissed her deeply. She moaned and felt the gush of cream hit her cunt then Cosivan sink all the way into her ass.

"Holy fuck," Cosivan moaned.

She couldn't take it. It was too much as her body exploded again and again. The orgasm just seemed to go on and on and then both men began to move. She was spent, done for and not a care in the world until both men started to fuck her so hard and fast she felt overwhelmed. Viktor came first, calling out her name.

"Holy shit. Oh God, baby, you're perfect. So fucking prefect," he said to her.

Behind her, Cosivan was thrusting into her ass and holding on to her hips. "I'm there, baby. Here I come," he shouted and she felt his dick somehow grow thicker and her insides felt so full she gasped. He shook behind her then held himself within her for a few seconds. She felt his mouth on her neck and shoulder as Viktor kissed her breasts, her neck, and then her lips.

"*Ya Lyublyu tyebya*," he whispered and Cosivan repeated the same words in Russian, too.

"What did you say? What does it mean?" she asked as Cosivan pulled slowly from her ass.

Viktor rolled her to her side, sliding his cock from her wet pussy. He cupped her cheeks. "It means we love you, sweet Nalia. Always and forever." He covered her mouth and kissed her then Cosivan did the same.

She smiled softly and looked at them. "I love you guys, too. Always and forever," she said and Cosivan didn't smile but instead caressed her thigh before he walked to the bathroom to grab a washcloth.

She lay there with Viktor until Cosivan returned and cleaned her up. She thought about what he said earlier and about the kind of men they all were and the professions they had. She loved them with all her heart and she would accept their responsibilities. She wouldn't give them a hard time or ask any questions, she would just love them whenever they were with her and be the kind of woman they needed and truly deserved.

Chapter 7

They were in town for less than a day when Cosivan and Viktor were attacked. It was after midnight when their plane arrived and they got to the waiting car. In communications with Nicolai, they decided to head to the club on Fuller Street. They made their way through the crowded bar area and into the back offices. Their men gave them an update on any problems they had with Lapella and Scarlapetti's crew making some drug deals at the club, and the increase in security since Zinc and Cobra were killed.

They gave their orders and then prepared to leave to go to the penthouse to get some sleep. Viktor was on the phone with Nina, making plans to see her in the morning and introduce her to a new security team. As they exited the offices and went back through the club, Cosivan spotted the angry expression on one man's face and then the response from others around him.

"Viktor," Cosivan said to him just as the one man attacked.

It was fast. The thrust of the knife against Viktor's chest and how quickly Viktor dropped the phone, shifted then countered. Cosivan saw the gun with the silencer on the one who went after him. He shifted, pulled the gun, and turned it on the man. The light sound, "pop, pop," brought the attackers to their knees and Cosivan and Viktor's men removed the other two. The small crowd of guards removed the bodies and Viktor and Cosivan hurried out the back door. It wasn't until they were in the car that Cosivan saw Viktor's angry expression and him holding his arm. Then came the sight of blood. "Fuck," Cosivan yelled.

He grabbed on to Viktor. "Are you okay? How bad?"

"It's not bad. Could have been worse if you hadn't yelled out my name. I was focused on talking to Nina. She sounded so upset but relieved I was in town to help."

One of the guards handed over a large first aid kit. Cosivan ripped Viktor's shirt and saw the large gash. "You'll need stitches. Luca," he called out to the driver.

"Already on my way, sir. How bad?" he asked.

"He's fucking lucky. Call Simon, find out who exactly those men were we took out in the club then have the men drop them on the fucker's doorstep," Cosivan said, the anger hitting him hard. Viktor could have been killed right there in front of him. He immediately thought about Nalia. He locked gazes with Viktor as he pressed the wad of gauze against the wound to suppress the bleeding. "Not a word to her. You don't tell her anything when we talk to Nalia. Understand?" Viktor demanded.

Cosivan nodded. "We're in a war, brother. Soldier mode for now on, got it?"

"Got it."

* * * *

Nalia knew that something was up. She overheard the angry tone as Chatham spoke into his cell phone in the hallway. It was the middle of the night and she could hardly sleep. She was worried about Cosivan and Viktor and missing them already.

"Fuck, what do you need us to do? Seriously, Cosivan? Maybe we need to be there, too. Perhaps place Nalia into a safe house with the family? We should be there. This is a war. Are you certain someone else is involved?" She heard only the one sided conversation and her heart raced. Something happened and she was worried.

She felt the arm go over her waist and Boian pulled her down. He snuggled his mouth against her neck and placed a leg over and between her thighs, caging her in. "No eavesdropping."

She swallowed hard. "Something is wrong," she whispered.

"Not your concern. Remember the rules Cosivan went over with you," he said firmly.

She remembered them. It was after they made love while he and Viktor held her between them. Cosivan made her promise to be strong, to be brave, and to trust in them to take care of her and each other. She was to ask no questions because they didn't want her to be part of this aspect of their lives. They wanted her safe, and untainted by the work they were forced to do in order to keep this dynasty, this family she was part of, alive and in control. They explained about the men who wanted to do the family harm and her father harm. In the last several weeks they each explained so much to her she understood exactly what she was becoming a part of. They spoke about the illegal and legal businesses, and how they owned and operated a few legitimate bars and restaurants, yet also engaged in criminal activity to make money and keep the control of territory that had been in the families for generations.

They also told her that they never killed just to kill or to make a point. They only killed in defending themselves as some tried to kill them. What they failed to remember, or maybe they chose to ignore, was that she knew what that felt like, too. She had been forced to kill in order to survive and not allow Scarlapetti's men get ahold of her and take her to Scarlapetti. She was a soldier, just like they were.

She listened anyway and heard Chatham's angry tone and then him say *fine*, and *okay, we'll take care of it.*

Then she felt Boian's mouth against her neck, suckling her skin before moving lower to her breast. He spoke against her skin.

"Open for me," he said.

"And for me," Dusty whispered, climbing up the bed to join them. She heard Chatham end the call and she looked toward him but then Dusty cupped her cheek and made her look at him before he lowered his mouth to kiss her.

Fingers pressed up into her cunt and she held her breath and fought to give in to their means of control and get lost in their touch, their bodies as they wanted her to. She wanted to demand to know what was really going on even though Cosivan, their leader, her leader, warned her not to. It had been an order. One that led to him taking her again in a slow, deep manner that forced her to realize she would do anything and give all of herself for each of them.

She moaned as the second finger thrust up into her cunt.

"Wider, bend your knees and slide you feet to your ass," Dusty commanded.

She lifted up with their assistance, widened her thighs, and felt the fingers stroke into her cunt then down over her anus. She was wet, and they moved the cream from pussy to anus.

"Do you know how much we love you?" Boian asked her. She looked at him as he thrust fingers deeper. Dusty caressed her thigh wider and kissed along her knee and inner calf.

"I think we should show her," Chatham said, joining them. She looked at him and he looked wild, needy.

"Chatham?" She said his name and he shook his head and gave her a firm expression. She wasn't to ask a thing.

Before she could protest Boian's fingers, slick with her cream, stroked over her anus and pressed in. In and out he thrust fingers, making her moan and then began to counterthrust.

"Ours, always and forever," Dusty told her then kissed her lips.

"Ours," Chatham said and then Boian pulled from her body and sat up. They moved her to her liking and she wound up over Boian and immediately she sank down onto his cock. A moment later, after only two thrusts she felt the cool liquid to her ass then Chatham grabbing ahold of her hips.

"I need you," Chatham said and she felt his cock slide into her anus slowly.

A firm hand to her cheek and hair and she locked gazes with Dusty.

"Me too," he said and he lowered her head to his cock and she immediately took him into her mouth.

They all began to move as one. She felt the connection, the depth of their love for her and hers for them. She loved their scents, their muscular bodies and even their dangerous professions and what they stood for. She couldn't help but feel the tears reach her eyes when she thought of Viktor and Cosivan and the fact they weren't here and could be in danger.

"Heaven, baby, you're heaven and make everything else disappear," Chatham told her.

"Fuck, I'm going to come. Holy God, it gets better and better," Dusty said to her.

She moaned and felt her body convulse around them as the tears rolled down her cheeks. *I love you guys. I need you. All of you. Help me to be strong for them, and the woman they need me to be.*

She swallowed as Dusty came first then Chatham and soon after Boian. Then she released a sigh and hid her eyes away from them as she kissed Boian and they took care of her as always.

* * * *

Chatham cleaned up and then came back to bed. He took Dusty's place beside Nalia and pulled her to him so Boian could get up. Both Dusty and Boian were probably wondering what the phone call had been about but they knew not to ask in front of Nalia. Besides, Viktor didn't want her to know what happened or how close he came to being more seriously hurt. She would find out when he returned to Salvation with an additional, new scar.

His chest tightened as he felt her damp cheeks and her slide her hand across her eyes to hide the tears.

"Nalia, are you okay?" he whispered.

Boian caressed her hair and head then kissed her temple.

"Baby?" he questioned.

"I'm fine," she whispered and hugged Chatham then began to scatter kisses along his chest.

Chatham winked at Boian, who looked concerned but then headed to the bathroom.

Chatham couldn't help but run his palms along her thighs and ass then pull her onto his chest as he rolled to his back. She lay half on top of him, his one thick thigh wedged between her thighs and warm pussy.

"I love being this close with you, skin to skin," he said and trailed a finger along her back then down the crack of her ass. She shifted slightly and her breasts lifted from against his chest then lowered again.

She snuggled closer then leaned up and kissed his chin. He tilted his head up and she kissed along his throat, loving the feel of her soft lips against him there. He slid his hands along her waist and felt how feminine and petite she was compared to him and his brothers. She didn't deserve to feel pain, to have had to go through what she did to survive when Karlicov was shot. He thought about Viktor and the stab wound. They needed to eliminate the problem, the threat, but Scarlapetti and Lapella were nowhere to be found, and now someone else was involved in hurting the family. Until they were dead, none of them could let their guards down.

"Are you okay, Chatham?" she whispered. He ran his hand along her ass and gave it a squeeze.

"More than okay with you in my arms," he said and she lifted up and licked her lips.

"Are you sure?"

He knew she heard the phone call and put two and two together. But Viktor and Cosivan were firm in their orders. She wasn't to know what happened. Cosivan was their commander, their leader and it was a direct order.

He held her hips and gave her a little shake. "Everything is fine, Nalia. No questions, remember?" he asked and she rolled her eyes and sighed. He shifted quickly, rolling her to her back and pressing her arms above her head. She gasped and then lowered down to lick across her nipple then tug on it. As he suckled then released it, she moaned.

"You know the rules. Don't push me, you won't be happy about the punishment," he said and her eyes widened like saucers.

He stared down into her dark blue eyes and gave her a wink.

"Let's get some more rest, we have a surprise for you," he told her and she gave a soft smile. He rolled off of her but continued to caress her skin.

"What is it?" she asked, keeping her arms above her head, waiting for his order to lower them. His cock hardened all over again. She was submissive, sexy, beautiful in so many ways. He trailed a finger from her lips to her nipples then her belly and cunt.

"You'll see, but only if you behave and listen. Now, close your eyes and rest." He leaned over and kissed her lips then Dusty joined them. He brought her hands to his chest and kissed her as Chatham snuggled up against her back. He slid his hand along her waist and held her with Dusty. He wished for so many things now that Nalia was part of their lives. But mostly he wished for them to all be together again soon, because being apart was definitely going to test Nalia's patience of the family rules.

* * * *

Nalia was smiling as Aspen pointed out a photograph of her men with their friends in a picture that hung on the wall in Casper's. She loved the place. It was fun, very country and everyone was friendly, even the sheriff. It was so crazy how these men, some of them government agents, state police and other types of law men, could be friends with members of the Russian mob. However, after a few little comments here and there it seemed like they all helped one another out and nothing illegal was done for favors. These were just men who served together, knew one another from their years in the service or had a family connection, and that was all it took for them to be close.

She shouldn't assume that her men did illegal dealings, but she wasn't stupid. They worked the system and in doing so they didn't follow rules, and laws. She knew enough to not ask them any questions about the business, but she had done a lot of research when her father had her trained and talked to her about some of the things he participated in. It was scary stuff, but also a way of life. It was a family business and operation and it appeared in more recent years they were going legit in so many ways. So she wondered how men like Scarlapetti could get away with their actions and how come some higher ups or leaders of all this stuff could do nothing? Men were being killed. She was abducted and going to be forced to have a man's baby.

She knew that certain ranks were involved and that it was a big deal to kill a boss. The more she thought about what Scarlapetti was capable of, the more she knew this world would be a better place without him.

"So, some more shopping after lunch?" Aspen asked.

"Sure," Nalia said and then she and Aspen walked over to one of the tables to talk. The men all seemed to be involved with some serious conversation and Nalia knew she wasn't supposed to listen in.

She was trying not to stare when she felt Aspen's hand cover hers.

"It gets easier. They're just protecting you," she told Nalia.

Nalia looked at her. Aspen was beautiful, young, and even pregnant. She was involved with multiple men, too, who were involved with things similar to Nalia's men.

"How do you do it? How do you come to this town whenever you feel like and feel safe and live a normal life? I mean when all the other things are going on."

"You mean the dangers? Hell, Nalia, I went through some crazy stuff to get here. I worked with some of those businessmen first hand that are now trying to take over the family's territory. It becomes a way of life and an understanding. My men are changing their ways in order to keep me and our growing family safe," Aspen said and covered her belly with her hand.

"They're going more legit and letting other men, single, experienced men handle the dangerous stuff while we expand our family. Your men will begin to do it, too. In fact, they already have."

"Have they? It doesn't seem like it."

"Well, haven't they told you about the clubs and restaurants they solely own?" Aspen asked.

"No. They don't tell me anything because they don't want me involved. This is all so new and Cosivan is very controlling and bossy. I think it's going to take a long time to figure the five of them out and what they expect from me and don't expect from me."

Aspen gave a soft smile. "You're young, and new to this type of relationship. It takes trust but patience, too. It will all come together. Don't be angry if they want to keep you separate from it all."

"Well, that's the thing. I don't want to be. I'm not weak or soft or incapable of handling the dangers or the business of what's going on. I don't like feeling shut out. I was made to feel unimportant, or like a separate responsibility all my life. My father had to pretend he was dead because I was born and no one could know I existed. The man my mother fell for she married out of convenience and stability and he wound up using her and killing her because of me, the child that should have never been born. If my father hadn't saved me from getting into trouble and began training me the way he did, then I wouldn't be here. It's in my blood. All of it comes so easy."

"You are more important than you even know. You are strong, I can tell that. Anyone with a brain could see you're capable. It's what made your men fall in love with you and also makes them so protective of you. Talk to them and make them understand that you want to be part of their business. Your father will be a help once you get to see him again when everything is safe. Be strong and be the woman your men need you to be and you will see that it will all work out. Besides, you have a friend in me now, too. We can help one another get over our men's protective measures in ensuring our safety." She gave Nalia a wink just as Storm came up behind Aspen and hugged her shoulders. Nalia watched as Aspen's eyes lit up, a smile formed on her lips and Storm ran his hand along Aspen's belly. He loved her and was very protective. *That's the kind of man women dream about.* Nalia had that times five.

* * * *

"We found her," Romeo told Vincent over the phone.

Vincent sat forward in his seat and felt his chest tighten.

"Go ahead," he said.

"She's in Texas, on a secluded piece of property. I've got men in the area and she's been spotted with three of Nicolai's main security soldiers. This will serve both of us well if you okay the move for me to take those men out. They own the clubs I've been trying to infiltrate," Romeo told him.

"You haven't been successful, from what I heard. My understanding is that Cosivan and Viktor removed your inside people and cleaned house. I believe you lost several men in your crew."

"And they will suffer for that."

"I don't know if this is wise. You heard the order from the bosses. I'm on my own with this challenge against the Russian mob bosses."

"You wanted Karlicov's daughter from the start. All of this happened because of the revenge you sought after he killed your brother and your cousin. Your hiding place in Florida is off the radar. You've got plenty of money. I'll help get her to you and you let me seek my own revenge on these fucking Russian assholes." Romeo was pissed off. That was obvious to Vincent.

"Fine. Take the chance, and if you're successful, then the deal is still on. I'll give you those twelve businesses you've wanted for years on the East Coast. They're yours if you can pull this off. I won't need it anyway. I'll be sitting back, enjoying my revenge."

"And enjoying one young, sexy piece of ass, I might add. Play your cards right and don't kill her, and she could serve you well for a very long time."

Vincent thought about that.

"Impress me, Romeo. I'll be waiting for my special package to arrive."

Vincent disconnected the call and then turned around to give full attention to his guest. The smell of cigar smoke filled the air.

"This better work or our deal is off, Vincent," Cornikup said to Vincent.

Vincent was so damn nervous about this guy. He had so much power and was sneaky, too. Karlicov didn't even know how much he was about to lose.

"It will work. They'll think it was Romeo and I who took her, and they'll hunt for us. You be sure to do your part and don't let them find me. Otherwise, I get to keep Nalia."

Cornikup smirked as he released another long breath of smoke.

"Watch yourself, Vincent. Like that I can end it all for you." He snapped his fingers and then stood up. His guards accompanied him off of the veranda and through the house.

Vincent took an unsteady breath. There was something about dealing with this guy that scared the crap out of him. Vincent hoped it was worth it. If Cornikup didn't kill Karlicov and the men guarding his daughter, then those men would come for Vincent, and all of these sacrifices were worth nothing at all.

* * * *

"Are you sure, Viktor?" Nina asked as she held his hand and he introduced her to the men who would be watching over her.

"They're good men, Nina. Well trained, very loyal to our family and personal friends of mine. It will be temporary, while my team and I work things out with Nalia and where we'll be living."

"But right now you'll be near this place, Salvation?" Nina asked.

"Yes. Not too far from where the house is that you'll be living in until this is over," the one man, Corona, added.

"Nina, I know you're scared, but you can trust these men. They're retired soldiers, and this is what they do. They were planning a bit of a vacation from everything and offered immediately for you to come with them. They knew Zinc and Cobra well. I trust them."

She looked at the one who Viktor said was their leader, Corona. He was big, very fit and muscular with tattoos, and looked ready for action. She didn't let on that she recognized two of the other men from the club she worked at. She'd met them separately and they had flirted with her. She didn't let on that she remembered them. She wouldn't want to send them the wrong signals.

"Okay, Viktor, I trust you."

Viktor gave her a nod and then he looked at Corona. "We'll be heading back to the house in Salvation tomorrow. Maybe in a few days once you're all settled in, you can bring her by the house to meet Nalia. I think it would be great for both of them," Viktor said to him.

"Whatever you think is right. We'll do our best to protect her."

Viktor gave his buddy's shoulder a slap. "I know you will. Keep me posted and good luck." Corona nodded and then helped Nina with her bags before they got into the SUV and headed to the airport.

* * * *

"We're getting closer. I fucking knew we would, Viktor. There was some chatter that Vincent was giving up some territory to Romeo on the east coast. There's some kind of deal going down in the next several days."

"What kind of deal, Cosivan?" Viktor asked. He took a seat in the chair in front of the desk. His heart was heavy for having to ship Nina off, but the good thing was that she wouldn't be too far from their own house where Nalia was. A thirty minute ride or so. He rubbed his arm where the stitches were. He missed Nalia. Tomorrow couldn't come fast enough.

"I'm going to pull some of our old buddies and put them on this. They have those connections in New York. Maybe they'll pick up on something."

"Good. I can't wait to get back to Salvation and see Nalia."

"And explain about those stitches," Cosivan said and raised his eyebrows up at him.

Viktor shrugged his shoulders. "She's going to be upset, but we'll keep her busy," he added and winked. Cosivan shook his head and barely smirked. That was Cosivan.

* * * *

Karlicov sat in the office talking to Nicolai.

"Don't worry, my friend, you'll get to see her soon. We're getting close and will take care of Lapella and Scarlapetti."

Karlicov nodded.

"It was all so unnecessary. I gave Nalia and Danella up to protect them. Danella is dead, and Nalia could have died, too. She is still in danger and always will be."

"But now she has her men. You made the right decision in allowing Team 13 to claim her and love her. It was meant to be."

"I didn't want her to have this life."

"Sometimes decisions are made for us and fate steps in. Cosivan and his men are well trained and one of the best teams we have. They will protect her with their lives."

Karlicov was silent as he thought about them. They were so much older. But Nicolai was right. There was no way of fighting fate. His daughter loved those men and it was obvious when Cosivan and Viktor talked to him and told Nicolai that they loved her, too.

"When all this is over we'll celebrate. After all, our friendship is now bound by blood as my nephew Viktor is part of Team 13," Nicolai said and winked.

Karlicov chuckled. "And to think how much trouble you first thought Viktor was going to be. He turned out to be the best soldier, the most loyal of all."

Nicolai smiled with pride.

"We were very lucky to be able to grab Viktor when my brother was killed. I almost lost him a few times to people, enemies that still live and breathe free."

"We'll always have our enemies, Nicolai. We can't let our guard down. They're out there, watching, waiting to strike and take what is dear from us. We must be diligent in protecting those so close to us."

Nicolai nodded. "We are doing the best we can."

"That we are, and you have your son, Viktor, and now I have my daughter, Nalia, to love and protect."

Nicolai gave a nod, but he couldn't fully smile. He had yet to find Malayna, a daughter he hadn't even known he had until it was too late. For all he knew she was dead, but there wasn't any proof. Her mother was murdered and Malayna taken from her home in Lozova in the Ukraine three years ago. She would be twenty-one now if she were still alive. His heart was heavy, his desire to find her still strong, yet all his leads failed to be successful.

Nicolai's phone rang and he answered it. "Really? he said and then smirked at Karlicov. "Take care of that and let me know when things are done." He disconnected the call.

"We got word from an unconfirmed source that Lapella and Scarlapetti are in Florida."

Karlicov clenched his teeth.

"My men are on it. If they are there, then this situation ends sooner than we hoped."

* * * *

Nalia couldn't help the tears that flowed the moment Cosivan and Viktor arrived. They hadn't even said they were coming home and as she got out of the bathroom after showering and saw them standing there in the bedroom she cried. Nalia ran across the room and Cosivan lifted her up into his arms and kissed her. He ran his hands all over her body as if seeing if she were real and she did the same to him. Of course she only had a shirt on. Cosivan's, actually. She nearly forgot how big Cosivan was and now he was back here with all of them.

"Sweet heaven, I missed this body," Cosivan told her and he caressed along her ass and then squeezed her to him. She hugged him tight and then smiled at Viktor, who waited not so patiently to kiss her hello next.

"We missed you, baby. God, you feel and smell so good," Cosivan said against her neck, suckling and kissing her skin. She giggled as she reached for Viktor. As he stepped closer she wrapped her arms around his neck and kissed him. Cosivan released her to Viktor and Viktor picked her up and kissed her deeply. She felt him sit on the edge of the bed and she pulled back to look at him. He smiled wide.

"I missed you so much," he told her and ran his hands along her arms and then under the shirt she wore.

"Hey, isn't this my shirt?" Cosivan asked, pulling on the hem, and she smiled then clutched it to her chest.

"Yes it is. I told you I missed you guys," she said.

"She sure did. She's been alternating between your shirts each night. But she never has them on long," Chatham teased and he reached out and stroked her cheek before he leaned down and kissed her. She lifted up to kiss him back and Viktor began to undo the buttons on her shirt.

"I need to see all of you. Damn, I'm going to kiss every inch of you, *sladkaya*," he said and then pressed her shirt away from her body.

"Hmmm…this is more like it," Cosivan said as he sat down next to Viktor, cupped her breast, and leaned forward to suckle her breast. She moaned softly, felt the tears in her eyes as she ran her fingers through his hair.

Viktor played with her other breast and she held his head there and exhaled.

They feasted on her slowly, enjoying her breasts while she rocked her hips on Viktor's lap. When both men pulled back she reached for Viktor's shirt and began to unbutton it. Cosivan stood up to undress.

The second Viktor pulled off his shirt she saw the bandage on his arm. She gasped and gripped his arms.

"What happened?"

He slid his arms around her waist and pulled her closer against his chest. He looked so serious her heart began to pound.

"It's nothing."

She looked at the others who were straight faced and still in the room watching over them, then she looked at Cosivan before she stared at Viktor. They all knew what this was. Something happened to him and no one told her. She sat up straighter. "What happened? Tell me now," she demanded.

"Later," Viktor said firmly and ran his hands along her thighs and her hips.

"Viktor."

"Shh, not now. Now I need you. To feel you in my arms and know you're safe and sound. I need to be inside of you where everything is perfect. Later, baby. Right now, I want to make love to my woman."

"I do, too," Cosivan said and lifted her up into his arms and kissed her.

He ran his hands all over her and she couldn't focus on anything but their sensual attack on her body. Cosivan lay down with her on top of him and kissed her deeply. She lifted her hips and he aligned his cock with her pussy and she immediately sank down on his cock. She lifted up when he released her lips and she moaned as she rocked back and forth on him.

"Sweet, sweet Nalia, I missed you so," he said as he held her hair and head, his forearm stretched out to brace her. When his hand landed on her throat as she rode him up and down she felt restrained, controlled and sexy. Cosivan was a master at seduction and she loved him.

She jerked only a moment when she felt the cool liquid against her anus. Then she shoved backward against Viktor's fingers and he stroked her immediately.

She and Cosivan moaned.

"Viktor, are you okay? It wasn't serious, was it?" She couldn't help but to ask. Cosivan used his thumb to stroke her throat but kept control of her with his hand on her neck and shoulder. She reached up and covered his forearm as she tilted her head back.

"No questions," Viktor said, pulling his fingers from her ass and replacing them with his cock.

He slid into her slowly and gripped her other shoulder and neck with one hand and hip on the other side with his other hand. Both men now had very possessive holds on her and she loved it. So much that after only a few strokes from both men she came, moaning and shivering as her orgasm hit her.

"That's right, Nalia. Remember the rules. All you need to worry about is loving us, being here for us, and completing us," Cosivan said. He and Viktor thrust into her pussy and ass, setting a rhythm that had her moaning and feeling overwhelmed.

"Oh God, please. Please," she moaned louder.

"Holy fuck, she loves being restrained. You look incredible, Nalia. So fucking perfect," Dusty chimed in.

"She sure does," Boian added and Chatham swore under his breath. Cosivan and Viktor continued their slow, deep thrusts and then she started pressing back and down then up and forward.

"Oh hell," Cosivan said and then he and Viktor increased their thrusts and Nalia couldn't move. She felt her body explode again and again and then finally Viktor and Cosivan came inside of her at the same time. They were panting for breath and she held on to Cosivan as Viktor slid from her ass. Cosivan rolled her to her back, pulling out of her pussy, and Chatham was there with a washcloth and towel to clean her up as both men scattered kisses along her skin.

"Damn, being away from you was pure hell," Viktor whispered and kissed her thigh.

"Worse than hell," Cosivan added and then kissed along her waist and then her belly. He used his fingers to stroke over her skin after Chatham cleaned her up. His lips touched her tattoo and then went along to where the stitches had been. "Nice and perfect. I barely see the marks," he told her.

She ran her fingers through Cosivan's hair. "Because my sexy, capable soldier knew what he was doing."

He lifted up and held her hips as he looked at her.

"I know how to do a lot of things, *malyshka*." He tickled her sides and she giggled until he stopped and stood up. Viktor took his place and pulled her against his side.

She immediately looked at the bandage and pulled her bottom lip between her teeth. She softly touched the outer part of the bandage on his upper arm.

"Nalia, let me hold you. I missed not being in bed with you." He pulled her close and she snuggled against him, absorbed his cologne as she kissed his skin and then Cosivan slid in behind her. He ran his palm along her ass and then her hip, before he kissed her shoulder.

"Ahh, now this is more like it," Cosivan said and the others chuckled.

"We'll see you guys in the morning," Boian told them and then each of them came over and kissed Nalia. First Boian, then Chatham, and finally Dusty. Her five American soldiers were safe and back together again. Everything felt perfect.

* * * *

"How is he really?" Chatham asked Cosivan.

Cosivan took a sip from his mug of coffee. "He needed thirty-five stitches, but you know Viktor," he replied. Chatham whistled low.

"My God, if that guy got him in the fucking chest," Dusty said.

"He didn't, so there's no need to think about that. He is fine and we took care of those assholes. What we need to do now is hope we get the phone call from Nicolai staying that Lapella and Scarlapetti are no longer a problem. Then we can make some concrete plans with Nalia," Cosivan said to them.

"She really likes it here in Salvation. She has plans with Aspen tomorrow and we already spoke with Corona and the guys about getting together with Nina so she can meet Nalia," Boian told him.

"That's great. I guess we can decide what we want to do and make some plans. Once this situation is resolved we might be able to work out having a place here as like a vacation home or weekend getaway or something," Chatham suggested.

"It's something to consider. Let's see what happens," Dusty added and Cosivan heard his cell phone ring. He glanced down and saw it was Nicolai.

"Fingers crossed, brothers," he said and then answered it.

* * * *

"Seriously?" Nalia asked and covered her mouth with her hand.

"Nalia, calm down."

She lifted her hand palm forward at Viktor and turned away from him.

He licked his lower lip and placed his hands on his hips.

"Just get into the shower," he told her and she shook her head. The water was running, they were going to shower then have breakfast with the others downstairs. He wrapped his arms around her midsection and pressed against her back. "I'm fine. It wasn't serious and it's not a big deal."

"Thirty-five stitches? You were stabbed, Viktor, and on top of that no one told me a damn thing." She turned around and he snagged her close before she could walk away. Her eyes landed on the bandage, now covered by waterproof tape.

Viktor ran his hand along her ass cheek and squeezed her to him. "I didn't want you to worry so I asked Cosivan to not tell you. Think about it. You would have been worried sick and then you couldn't see me to see that I'm perfectly fine."

"I want to know how it happened. Every damn detail, Viktor," she stated firmly. He raised one of his eyebrows up at her and she pulled her lip tight and then lowered her eyes.

Smack.

He spanked her ass. "Get in the damn shower. I'll explain everything," he said and then got into the shower with her and helped her get lathered up with soap. He explained in little detail about the night they arrived. He should have left that part out, she was even more furious. But as he explained what happened and how they were able to handle the men responsible she seemed to get quiet.

"You need to learn that we can't tell you about every little detail of our jobs. If we get some sort of injury or scar, you don't need to know how."

"That's not really fair. It means you can keep secrets from me," she said and then rinsed the conditioner out of her hair. He turned her around and pressed her against the wall. He lifted her arms above her head and she gasped. Keeping a firm expression, he stared down into her gorgeous dark blue eyes.

"I love you, Nalia. I've never said those words to any other woman ever. I have gone through things in my life I will probably never tell you about. Things that changed me, made me the man I am today. Letting go, having a woman like you who cares and who loves with all her heart is going to take some time getting used to. Can you please give me some slack here? I'm stubborn, used to handling this shit on my own and keeping things inside of me. I don't trust easy, and I can count on both hands how many people I fully trust with my life, and with yours. So I'm only going to tell you this once. When I say no questions, it means no questions."

He couldn't tell if she was accepting, upset, or what. But then she held his gaze and nodded.

"I love you, too. I appreciate your honesty and that's all I really want. To know that you are okay. I've been through a lot, too. I never told a man I loved him, never mind five men. I gave my body to you, and my heart and soul. That means you're part of me. So if you hurt, I hurt. If you're happy, then I'm happy. It's something new for both of us."

"Ya lyublyu tyebya, my Milaya." He kissed her deeply then brought her arms over his shoulders and hugged her tight. She kissed his neck once he released her lips and he knew that she was the most important person in his life. He would love her forever. He would do everything in his power to keep her safe, to protect her from harm and from ever feeling fear or pain again.

Chapter 8

"Vlladim, I need security to be top notch. Although I don't expect there to be any surprise visitors, I need the chopper on standby as well as the jet in case I need a quick getaway. We won't go into Moscow unless it is necessary. I'd rather do her training here, in the States. It will be too much of a hassle getting her through security to go out of the country. Not until she is completely submissive," Cornikup told him.

Vlladim nodded his head and then glanced at the young woman kneeling on the floor. Cornikup caressed her hair. And smiled at his prisoner.

"You will have some company soon enough. Nalia will be here by tomorrow and I expect you to teach her the rules," he said to the young woman.

"Yes, Cornikup. I will do as you say," she whispered. Vlladim couldn't help but to look over her sexy body. She had long brown hair, deep blue eyes and was sweet and submissive. Cornikup trained her to be that way and he couldn't help but to wish he could get his hands on her. Vlladim wondered when Cornikup would take her virginity and taint the woman and her family. If he wasn't up for the job then Vlladim would do the dirty work. He licked his lips.

"Ahh, Vlladim, you look at my prize, my revenge with such desire in your eyes. You have been such a loyal protector." He caressed the young woman's hair and then ran his fingers along her collarbone then her breast. She shivered and remained straight faced. She was so obedient now, even Vlladim could hardly remember when she had to be beaten into submission.

"She is quite beautiful, and you have been so patient with her, and have trained her to be obedient as our ancestors before us had with their women."

"And I will do the same to Nalia with your help. We will see how long it will take to break Nalia down, considering your sources say she is quite resourceful."

"She will need to be restrained at all times. I will help in every way I can."

"Good, stay on top of things and let me know as soon as she is in our men's possession. In the interim, do you know if Nicolai and Karlicov found Lapella and Scarlapetti as we planned?"

"They should be infiltrating the mansion as we speak. I'll hear from my men who are in Salvation and see if they feel confident in grabbing Nalia."

Cornikup smiled. He cupped the young woman's chin.

"Nicolai will never know that I have you, just as Karlicov will never know it is me who has his daughter, Nalia."

* * * *

Cosivan, Boian and Dusty had left for Florida along with other members of the organization. They had concrete proof on the whereabouts of Vincent and Romeo and wanted to be there to take them down. Nalia wasn't too happy about them leaving and they didn't tell her why, so she wouldn't be scared. Cosivan, Viktor and Chatham remained behind, hoping to give Nalia the good news shortly.

"Anything yet?" Storm asked Cosivan as they stood outside of the boutique in town while Aspen and Nalia shopped.

"They were getting ready to go into the estate about thirty minutes ago," Chatham told them.

"Then this will all be over very soon," Winter replied.

"Then you guys can look into purchasing that house you've been holding up in as a vacation home. I know Aspen will be thrilled to have Nalia around," Storm said to Cosivan, Viktor, and Chatham.

"And maybe marry that woman and start a family? That way our little one has a playmate as we expand this family," Winter said and they chuckled.

Cosivan looked toward the boutique. He could imagine himself living here part time with his brothers and Nalia. He couldn't even imagine her pregnant with their baby, but anything seemed possible now that Nalia was part of them. She changed their world and turned their lives upside down. He thought he was a heartless bastard destined for loneliness and a life of violence. He craved it, lived for it, and even though he didn't need to engage in violence as much as years ago, it seemed Nalia was making him less and less interested in this aspect of his profession. Perhaps like Storm and his men, Cosivan and his team could make some changes too?

* * * *

Nalia was laughing as Aspen tried on a sexy dress and ran her hands along the small bump of her belly. She couldn't help but smile and hope to one day have her men's babies as well. She thought about the dangers but one look at Aspen and she knew that the men would protect them all. This family went beyond blood, and would continue to expand with the years to come.

"I'm going to try this skirt and blouse on. I'll meet you up front," Nalia said and Aspen nodded as she continued to look at the rack of clothing in the boutique.

When Nalia entered the hallway and the back changing room she thought she felt a breeze coming from down the hallway. It was a little warm today and the owners probably opened up the back door for some fresh air.

She slid into the dressing room and began to change. She glanced at her body in the mirror and looked down at the sexy lingerie she bought to surprise her men with tonight. She couldn't help but be ecstatic. She hadn't chosen a black set, but instead a pretty set in yellow that would look amazing against her tattoo.

She placed it down onto the bench and pulled the skirt and blouse on over her black bikini lace set. She fixed her hair and tried to see how the outfit looked in the mirror but it was tight in there, so she slipped on her sandals and headed to the larger mirror in front of the other empty rooms since no one was inside but her.

As she began to turn she heard a noise and then felt the prick to her neck just as the large man grabbed ahold of her and covered her mouth. "Don't scream, Nalia, or I'll kill the pregnant bitch."

She instantly knew she couldn't put Aspen and the baby in danger and as she wondered who this guy was she felt the room begin to spin. He stuck her with something. What was it? But as he moved her she felt her legs give out and then him lift her up into his arms as if she were light as a feather before heading down the hall and out the back door into the sunlight. She couldn't get her voice to work and as he got into the back seat of a van the driver drove off and darkness overtook her vision.

* * * *

"Thank God, you got them. It's over then?" Cosivan said into the phone and the others around them began to celebrate.

"I have to tell Nalia," Chatham said and started heading into the boutique. Cosivan followed, excitement in his heart at knowing the danger, the fear was finally over and they could move on with their lives with Nalia.

Then they heard Aspen yell to them from the front door. "Nalia is gone. Something is wrong."

Cosivan yelled into the phone and ran with the others inside. They were looking in the dressing room and saw the back door open and a needle on the rug.

"Oh fuck, someone took her," Storm yelled and pulled out his cell phone.

"Get the surveillance tapes," Zin said to Viktor.

Cosivan yelled into the phone. "Someone took Nalia. She's gone."

Cosivan clenched his teeth and felt anger like he never felt before fill his heart.

"They're dead. Whoever they are, I'm going to kill them with my bare fucking hands."

Chapter 9

"No. No more, you're going to kill her, Vlladim. She'll listen. I'll get her to listen," Malayna begged of him as she grabbed on to Vlladim's arm and hugged him to her so he would stop striking Nalia. Malayna was getting tired of the beatings, of Nalia screaming for help then defying them and not giving in to the control. It had been weeks since she arrived here and she knew that Nalia would rather die than give in to Vlladim and Cornikup's control.

Vlladim grabbed onto Malayna and pressed her up against the wall. He was breathing through his nose and clenching his teeth. "You know better than to touch me without permission."

He wasn't a huge man but he was muscular, trim, and crazy in the head. She feared him more than she feared Cornikup. She had hoped that if Nalia had gotten here that they could talk and get through this together. She had been alone for three years, but in those three years she learned so much about Cornikup and how to destroy him. She would get that chance someday and somehow. She would do whatever it took to get that opportunity.

He reached up and grabbed her face. She tilted her head back, heard Nalia moaning in the background as she lay on the rug in the bedroom.

"You have not been able to convince her or teach her the rules since she arrived here three weeks ago. She learns the hard way, just as you did three years ago, Malayna."

Malayna remembered those weeks of resisting and fighting. They beat her down physically and then emotionally. It wasn't until she lay on the ground bloody and battered that she learned the truth behind who these men were and why they killed her mother and took her when she was eighteen. Cornikup thought she was unconscious as he talked to Vlladim about his revenge. So she did have a father, and his name was Nicolai Merkovicz, and he was a main boss in the Russian mob.

"I want to keep trying. I know she is defiant now, as I was, Vlladim, but she will learn, and then be ready for Cornikup and whatever plans he has for her."

Vlladim caressed her cheek and then ran a finger over her lip. She forced herself not to shudder at his touch. She knew he wanted her and she feared that Cornikup would give her to Vlladim for being so loyal and for wanting her as his own.

If that day came, it would be her last day on this earth. She would kill him when he wasn't expecting it, even if it meant him taking from her body, and making her move when he was weak and inside of her.

She lowered her eyes. "Please, sir," she said to him.

She felt his cock against her groin and then she felt him cup her breasts. She gasped and looked up, locking gazes with him. He clenched his teeth. "One day soon you are going to be mine, Malayna. I have wanted you since day one. I'm not weak, nor will I be tricked. Get her to cooperate, or you will suffer some of her pain as well."

He lowered her feet to the ground but not before squeezing her ass and giving it a smack. She jumped away from him and he smirked but looked at her with evil and lust in his eyes. It wouldn't be long now. She had to get Nalia to cooperate so she could survive. Malayna was running out of time.

* * * *

Nalia felt the warm washcloth against her battered skin. She ached everywhere and the cuts and bruises were raw and painful. She didn't want to move.

"Just lay still, Nalia."

"Malayna?" she whispered. She had been the one to take care of her after Vlladim's beatings. Nalia didn't know what was going on, who these men were, and where she was. Malayna had whispered things to her but she didn't know if she were dreaming or if those things were real.

"Who are you?" Nalia asked her as she blinked her eyes to try and open them but they hurt, too.

"I told you, Nalia. You need to listen to me and to learn the rules. It's been three weeks since Vlladim brought you here."

"Three weeks?" She felt the tears roll down her cheeks. Why hadn't her men come for her? Who was this man who held her captive?

"You need to listen to me. The men you say you love will never find you. They can't and you need to keep quiet about loving them. If Cornikup and Vlladim find out then they'll do worse to you. They'll take from your body. They have to think you are a virgin still," she whispered and looked around to be sure no one could hear her.

Nalia swallowed hard.

"How do you know? How long have you been here?"

"Three years," she whispered.

"Three years. Oh my God. Oh God, no. No," she cried, feeling sick and weak.

"Shh, please, Nalia, listen to me. They'll take you out of the country as soon as they can and you're trained. I'm not going to last much longer. Vlladim is going to want me for himself and I feel that Cornikup wants you. He'll release me to Vlladim for him being so loyal."

"Oh God, Malayna. Who is this Cornikup and why does he want me?"

"I heard him say revenge. Your father Karlicov killed someone in his family, a brother I think, and Nicolai gave the order. Cornikup retaliated and sent a man, his main guard to kill your father, but Nicolai's brother, Jacob, was there with his son, and killed Nicolai's brother. But then Jacob's son, who was a teenage boy, killed Cornikup's main guy. He sought revenge against Nicolai but there was no one he was close to. Then he found out about my mother. That's when he sent Vlladim to kill her and to take me."

"Why?"

Malayna swallowed hard and whispered to her. "I am Nicolai's daughter."

Nalia gasped. "You have a sister, and a cousin." Nalia began to explain and Malayna was shocked to learn about Aspen and to also learn about Viktor.

"He is one of my men. He must have been the teenager that killed Cornikup's main guy back then."

"Oh my God, we can't let anyone know. None of it matters. They will never find you just like my father never found me. I don't even know if he knows I exist."

"You can't think that way. You have to keep fighting," Nalia said to her.

She shook her head. "Nalia, don't make the mistakes I did. Don't plan and hope on a possibility of being rescued like I once had. They aren't coming for you. No one will find you or know where to find Cornikup. I've been a prisoner for three years. Three years, Nalia. I finally understand that my life is over and I am going to die here. Be smart and learn the rules quickly. This is your new life, unless you decide you are willing to push Vlladim and Cornikup to the point of killing you. Then that will be your destiny, just as I have stated mine."

"We can't give up, Malayna. Your father is helping my men, your cousin find me, and they will find us. My men and the others in the family are American soldiers. They're resourceful and they love me. I know they're coming, and when they do, we need to be ready to help them."

"I don't think I have any more fight inside of me, Nalia. I was eighteen when they killed my mother in front of me and then took me away from the only home I ever knew."

"They killed my mother in front of me as well."

"What did you do?"

"I killed the man who did it. I can help us get out of here."

"No, no, you can't and that will make Vlladim even angrier. Aren't you tired of getting beaten and touched?" she asked.

"I will continue to fight. It's in my blood to not give in to the enemy, Malayna, and it is in yours, too."

"I can't."

"You will, and when the time comes. When my men come for me, I'll need you to help me. To get me a loaded gun, any weapon you can."

"And what? Fight off Vlladim and Cornikup and their men on your own?"

"And kill them, because I was trained by my father, and survived his enemies wanting to kill me before. I will survive now. I've got lucky Team 13 on my side, and on yours, too."

* * * *

"Mexico. They are located on a heavily guarded compound in Mexico," Nicolai addressed the large group of men along with Karlicov.

"Where? When can we leave? How many?" Boian asked, sitting forward in his seat.

Nicolai held up his hand and looked around the room at all the men gathered there.

"This is a great enemy of mine and Karlicov's. Viktor, he is the one responsible for giving the order to kill your father."

Viktor clenched his teeth and his brothers looked cold as ice. They were exhausted, had very little sleep, and were at their wits' end over the abduction of Nalia. Three and a half weeks had passed. The surveillance tapes at the boutique in Salvation revealed a man who they identified as one of Cornikup's soldiers. That information came from Star and his team of men on the hunt for a man named Vlladim they wanted to kill. They were part of the Mulicheck family, a second in command under Nicolai.

He explained more about the men they were hunting and then about Star, Krane, Luca, and Border. They would be going in first, leading the infiltration of the compound.

"We want to be there and go in," Cosivan said, standing there with his arms crossed and ready to kill.

"And you all will. We have to ensure that this situation ends there in Mexico. I will have other members of the extended family on high alert. The plane leaves in thirty minutes. You will work together with Star and his team to accomplish this mission. I leave you, Star and Storm in charge of this, Cosivan. Your military backgrounds will be quite useful in putting an end to this situation once and for all," Nicolai told him.

Cosivan, Star and Storm nodded their heads and then Viktor looked at Karlicov. "We will bring back your daughter. She never should have been taken from us."

"You bring back your wife. You do everything you can to protect her and ensure that nothing like this ever happens again."

* * * *

Nalia cried out as Vlladim pulled the chains that were attached to her wrists. She was bloody and battered, but resisted less and less and played somber and weak a little more each day. She needed these men to believe they were breaking her down as Malayna told her to. It was too hard not to shake or feel disgusted when Cornikup touched her and petted her hair. He treated her like a pet, an animal, and she thought of all the ways she could and would kill the fuck.

She tested the amount of give in the chain and whether or not she had enough leeway to hold a gun and shoot it with some precision. She kept contemplating different plans and acting them out in her head with all the scenarios that could take place. She had to put into account her battered body, the bruised if not broken ribs, and her more recent injury, her sprained ankle. Kicking that piece of crap Vlladim in the nuts had felt really good, but it cost her.

"A few more weeks and if you submit and accept your fate, I can do away with the chains," he said and brought the links up to her cheek and caressed her bruised jaw. He looked at the gap in the stupid smock they made her wear and he licked his lips at the sight of her breasts. They were bruised too from the strokes against her skin by Vlladim. But at least they didn't try to touch her sexually. Not until today as Cornikup licked his lips and stroked a finger into the gap.

She shivered at the feel of his thick finger pressing into the cup of her bra. She stared at him, trying to maintain eye contact as he demanded, but not show her disgust or the daggers she wanted to throw at him. Again, as he watched her, got aroused by it, she stared straight faced and contemplated a plan. She relaxed. She wasn't such a patient woman. That she had a temper, a fire in her that kept rising up, and she needed to tamp it down and tell herself to wait. *Just wait, and this sicko's time will come.*

He trailed his finger from her breasts to her throat then her chin, grasping it as he looked down at her. Kneeling on the floor like some servant really pissed her off. *I'm going to kill you the moment I have an opportunity and I don't even care if I die.*

She had to sit up completely on her knees and raise her chin as he pulled harder. She was losing balance and shifted forward, having to place her hands on his knees for support. His teeth clenched. He closed his eyes and inhaled.

"Sweet, sweet Nalia. My plans keep changing for you. I thought I would just keep you as my pet and then eventually kill you, but it seems Vlladim wants Malayna for himself." He licked her lips and she clenched her eyes closed, both disgusted and shocked at what he was doing to her and also at his plans for Nicolai's daughter. The man was as good as dead if she could just get her and Malayna out of here.

He gripped her head a little more firmly and then pressed his mouth to hers. The forceful kiss and plunge of his tongue had her gripping his thighs and pushing back.

When he released her lips she felt like vomiting.

His eyes never left hers.

"Still resistant to your fate." He nodded and when she went to see who was behind her strong arms gripped her around the waist and set her on her feet. Vlladim grabbed her chains and tugged tight.

"Seems you need more discipline."

Her heart hammered in her chest as he dragged her along, limping from her sprained ankle and not caring at all. Anger, so deep, so dark, pooled in her belly.

I can't take this much longer. I won't let them rape me and break me down. I need an opportunity. Please, one opportunity to take them out and then I don't care what happens to me.

* * * *

Night had set and the compound was surrounded by a dozen men. All Special Forces and Navy SEALs, all members of the Merkovicz family. Cosivan looked at Star Mulicheck, the leader of Krane, Luca, and Border. They were very lethal men. The kind of men Cosivan and his team respected and trusted with Nalia's life. The fact that they were working together was rare. These men hardly socialized. They were warriors, special operations men who only did heavy shit like this when the family called upon them. Funny thing was, they lived all over the place and rarely settled in one place too long. They did have investments in various clubs and other businesses they had other people run. They were powerful, wealthy men and resourceful.

"Okay, Star, you're running this operation, our woman's life is in your hands. Are you certain the count of guards is accurate and all security around the perimeter can be disengaged?"

"They won't hear us coming in. They won't know we're even in there until it's too late. The concern is locating where Nalia is once we're inside. It's not such a small place. We take out everyone, no witnesses, no evidence left behind," Star warned as if Cosivan and his men were not so experienced. It didn't really piss Cosivan off. He would be saying the same thing if he was leader of this.

"No evidence, but can't promise not to make these fuckers suffer," he added and Star nodded.

He spoke into his mic.

"On my count of three, we begin," he said and they heard the command loud and clear through their earpieces. They would be in constant communication so that when Nalia was located they all could do whatever was necessary to get to her. He glanced at his brothers and their angry, ice cold expressions. They were desperate to find Nalia and bring her home. Desperate to hold her in their arms and make this up to her. They let their guard down, and here they were nearly two months of searching, of longing to have her back and coming up empty handed with every search, and now they found her. Or so he hoped.

* * * *

"Take a sip of this. It will help," Malayna whispered as she helped Nalia drink.

"Oh God, what is this?" she asked her. It tasted disgusting.

"It's a bunch of herbs and things that help numb pain but also give energy to your system like a reboot."

"Reboot? I want to lay here and not move at all."

"No, you need to drink and be ready. Vlladim is getting impatient. I fear he's going to try to touch me, or worse. I saw how Cornikup was touching you. He wants you, Nalia. We have to make a move and try to escape."

Nalia's eyes widened. "My damn ankle is worse."

Malayna looked down.

"It may be broken. It's awfully swelled up and way worse than yesterday. We'll figure it out."

She touched Malayna. "We'll have to kill them," she whispered and Malayna swallowed hard.

"Then I need a gun. This knife won't do," she said and showed Nalia the knife.

Suddenly they heard arms going off.

"Take this," Malayna said to her and gave her the knife.

"Where are you going?"

"To try and find a weapon and see what is happening."

As she turned, the door burst open.

Malayna stood up as Vlladim headed toward her and Cornikup stomped toward Nalia. They had guns and looked panicked.

"Cornikup?" Malayna said aloud as Vlladim grabbed her arm.

"We need to move. Now."

"Get up. They won't find you. I'll kill you before I let them ruin my plans." Cornikup struck Nalia across the mouth and then gripped her, pulling her up to stand. Her ankle gave out and she cried out in pain. She heard Malayna scream and saw Vlladim dragging her toward another set of doors.

"Fuck you," Nalia screamed out and used both hands and arms as a bat and slammed into his arms. The gun fell from his hands and she lost her balance and fell to the ground. She saw the knife and gripped it but the boot landed against her shoulder and she fell back down.

She scrambled over, grabbing the knife and as Cornikup ripped her dress, pulling her up off the ground, she struck the knife at his face. He hollered and grabbed his face. She used both hands, still locked in chains, to swing the knife at him again and again. She cut his stomach through the shirt he wore and then somehow got up on her knees and lunged for him again.

He went down and they scrambled for the knife. She felt the cut to her side as she screamed in anger and pain but kept fighting. They were rolling and she somehow wrapped her chains between her wrists around his neck. She pulled back. His hands gripped the chain to try and stop her from choking him. With the little strength she had left she pulled back. He landed hard on top of her, back to her chest. She wrapped her legs around his midsection, squeezing, clenching her teeth as she pulled the one around his neck tighter. This was it. It was either he died or she died.

She heard the gurgling and him shaking then the crack, just as the doors burst open and her strength left her. She thought she was going to die. That the ones entering were Cornikup's men but then she heard her name.

"Nalia!" Viktor's voice filled the dim room and then there was gunfire echoing in the background and her men shoving Cornikup off of her.

"Oh God, she's alive. She's alive," Viktor said into his wrist. Chatham cupped her cheeks and she moaned in pain.

"Fuck, she's bleeding in multiple places," he said and then more light shown on her.

"She has stab wounds," Boian said.

They were all dressed in black, looking like military insurgents. She blinked her eyes and shook. Then other men were standing there.

"The place is clear. Our men are on foot outside the perimeter for anyone who could have escaped."

"Malayna. You have to save Malayna," she said and grabbed on to Viktor.

"We need to get the hell out of here, now," another voice she didn't recognize chimed in.

"Let's get her up. We can look over her injuries on the plane."

She grabbed on to Cosivan as she felt her head spinning and weakness beginning to overtake her. There was another man next to him. She clenched her teeth.

"You must find Malayna and save her."

"Who the hell is she talking about?" the other man asked.

"Cosivan, she's Nicolai's daughter," she told them.

"What? His daughter is here?" another man said.

"Nalia, Nicolai doesn't have a daughter besides Aspen," Viktor said to her.

"He does. It has to do with your father and the whole reason behind the revenge and the killings."

"Malayna is here? You're certain?" this other man asked. She didn't know if she should reply.

"Nalia, this is Star, he's part of a team Nicolai sent in to rescue you with us. Trust him," Cosivan told her.

"It's her. I swear it is. Vlladim wants her and took her just as Cornikup came in here trying to take me."

"We have to find her," Star said then stepped away and spoke into his mic.

"Let's get you out of here," Chatham said, lifting her into his arms.

She held on to him and felt her other men touching her, caressing her. She looked at Boian and Cosivan. "Go with them. Vlladim is evil, and Malayna won't be able to fight him."

* * * *

Malayna was trying to slow Vlladim down as she fell several times along the border of the property. She could still hear gunfire and then the sound of yelling.

When she heard her name, she instinctively screamed out. "Help!"

Vlladim struck her and she fell to the ground. When he reached for her she kicked at him and used what strength she had to fight him off.

She heard her name again and it sounded like it was coming closer.

"Help!" she cried out and Vlladim grabbed her shirt and yanked her up but she stayed on her knees, making him struggle. She heard more yelling and turned to see men running toward them.

Vlladim gripped her throat and she thought he was going to kill her right here. She slammed her hands at his arms. "This isn't over. I will hunt you until you're mine again." He struck her so hard she fell back onto the ground, feeling dizzy and out of sorts.

"Malayna?" She heard her name and saw a man in black with bright blue eyes staring down at her. She tried to move and couldn't. She was so dizzy. He placed his hands over her belly.

"Don't move. We're here to help you. Nalia sent us," he said to her and Malayna felt the tears fill her eyes.

Then other men were there, too. "This is her? What happened to Vlladim?" some other man asked.

"He took off that way," the blue-eyed guy said as he put a flashlight over her and checked her injuries.

"Cosivan and Luca went after him," another man said and he leaned down. "Malayna, I'm one of Nalia's men. You're safe now. We're going to bring you home to your father."

"My father?" she asked.

The man with the blue eyes nodded. "We'll get you there. My men and I will ensure your safe return to Nicolai," he said and then reached for her to pick her up.

She heard them talking as he carried her in his arms and she lay against his shoulder. She felt numb, yet safe until she heard one of the men talking. "They can't find him. Vlladim got away."

"Send them back. We need to get the hell out of here, daylight is on our asses," he told them in a commanding tone as he carried her through the darkness and to an awaiting vehicle. It was over. She was finally free.

* * * *

Nicolai fell slowly to his chair as he listened to Star speak to him on the phone. Karlicov was there with him as word came in that Nalia was alive and safe. They needed to stop for medical attention for her. It was pretty bad.

"Nicolai, Nalia found Malayna. She was being held prisoner all these years by Cornikup and this guy, Vlladim."

"What?" he asked and looked at Karlicov.

"Oh my God," Karlicov said and stood up, placing his hand on Nicolai's shoulder. He knew his right hand man knew the story and how long they searched for her. Star and his team had gone on various hunts that led to nothing at all.

"Star, it's her? You're certain?"

"Yes, sir, it seems to be her. She has a concussion and some bruising. She's insistent on remaining with Nalia, because Nalia saved her life."

"How is Nalia? What are her injuries?" he asked.

"She has knife wounds, a broken ankle, and lots of cuts and bruising. Cornikup and Vlladim worked her over good. We're about ten minutes out from a medical facility," Star told them.

"And Cornikup and Vlladim?" Nicolai asked as Karlicov gripped the desk.

"Vlladim disappeared as we stopped him from taking Malayna, and Cornikup is dead."

"So you got him? It's over?" Karlicov said.

"Nalia killed him," Star said and Karlicov lowered his head. Nicolai was in shock.

"Bring our daughters home safely, Star. Thank everyone for us as well."

Epilogue

Nalia gasped and then moaned loudly before she felt the warm, large hands caressing her skin. "You're safe, *Milaya*," Cosivan whispered.

Her mind began to process what was going on and where she was. The sounds were somewhat familiar as machines beeped and the scent of antiseptic filled her nostrils. She blinked her eyes open and saw all the people there. She felt the tears emerge. It was real. She was rescued. She was safe. Nalia tried to see clearly but this groggy feeling consumed her and her head and body felt so heavy. Then came the sound of her father's voice. She turned slightly, feeling an ache but then she felt his hand on her shoulder.

"You amaze me, Nalia. So strong, so persistent to fight and fight and stay alive." He kissed her forehead and she felt the tears fill her eyes. She loved her father so much. That thought made her think of Malayna.

She gasped. "Malayna," she said and went to push up and cringed.

"No, lay still," multiple voices said to her. She blinked her eyes and saw her men, and then the door to the room opened and two very large men came walking in with Malayna. She had a bandage on her head, and a swollen lip. The guys moved out of the way and Malayna began to cry. So did Nalia.

She got to the bed and hugged Nalia. "Thank you. You saved my life and I could never pay you back," she said.

"Sure you can," Nalia whispered.

Malayna pulled back and looked at her. "How?"

"By being my friend, besides my family."

Malayna smiled and hugged her again.

"Friends for life," she said and Nalia smiled then cringed.

"What's going on in here? She can't have this many people here." The doctor came into the room and slowly everyone began to leave. Nalia closed her eyes, feeling so tired and just heavy like she could lay here and sleep forever.

She felt the fingers stroking her hair and then lips press against her cheek.

"You need to rest," Boian said to her and she gave a soft smile. She looked at all her men who gathered around her now. Viktor stood on the other side next to Chatham and they both had a hand on her arm. Dusty and Boian were on the left side both caressing her skin and Cosivan stood at the end of the bed, arms crossed and very serious.

"I missed you so much. I was so scared that I would never see you again." The tears fell and her men looked serious and hard.

"We never should have let our guard down," Chatham said to her.

"No, Chatham, it was out of your control. No one, not even Nicolai, knew about Cornikup and his plan of revenge. I knew you would eventually find me, that you would never give up."

"Did you really, or are you just saying that?" Boian asked her. She thought about it a moment and gave a wise guy expression. Even though she planned on fighting until she died if necessary, she did hold on to a hope that her men would search and rescue her.

"Hello? You're my American soldiers. Of course you would find me. Besides, you're my lucky charms," she said and closed her eyes.

She felt the kiss to her lips and blinked one eye open to see Viktor. "Your lucky charms? What happened to number thirteen not being lucky for you?" he teased.

"Not being lucky? The number thirteen means everything to me. I was born on Friday the 13th. I found out about my father on my thirteenth birthday. You found me after thirteen weeks on the run. I can go on and on, but the very best is so obvious. It's the five of you.

You're my everything. The loves of my life, my own personal bodyguards, my American soldiers, and my lucky Team 13."

She closed her eyes and smiled softly. "Yup, I'd say thirteen is indeed the luckiest number I've ever known."

THE END

WWW.DIXIELYNNDWYER.COM

ABOUT THE AUTHOR

People seem to be more interested in my name than where I get my ideas for my stories from. So I might as well share the story behind my name with all my readers.

My momma was born and raised in New Orleans. At the age of twenty, she met and fell in love with an Irishman named Patrick Riley Dwyer. Needless to say, the family was a bit taken aback by this as they hoped she would marry a family friend. It was a modern day arranged marriage kind of thing and my momma downright refused.

Being that my momma's families were descendants of the original English speaking Southerners, they wanted the family blood line to stay pure. They were wealthy and my father's family was poor.

Despite attempts by my grandpapa to make Patrick leave and destroy the love between them, my parents married. They recently celebrated their sixtieth wedding anniversary.

I am one of six children born to Patrick and Lynn Dwyer. I am a combination of both Irish and a true Southern belle. With a name like Dixie Lynn Dwyer it's no wonder why people are curious about my name.

Just as my parents had a love story of their own, I grew up intrigued by the lifestyles of others. My imagination as well as my need to stray from the straight and narrow made me into the woman I am today.

Enjoy *The American Soldier Collection 13: Her Lucky Number Thirteen* and allow your imagination to soar freely.

For all titles by Dixie Lynn Dwyer, please visit
www.bookstrand.com/dixie-lynn-dwyer

Siren Publishing, Inc.
www.SirenPublishing.com

Lightning Source UK Ltd.
Milton Keynes UK
UKHW011319041019
351005UK00014B/1002/P